THE CUR SONG

an alien's quest for meaning on the strangest planet in the universe

Bob Lockyer

© 1999 by Robert K. Lockyer. All rights reserved.

Printed in the United States of America.

Packaged by WinePress Publishing, PO Box 428, Enumclaw, WA 98022. The views expressed or implied in this work do not necessarily reflect those of WinePress Publishing. Ultimate design, content, and editorial accuracy of this work are the responsibilities of the author.

No part of this publication may be reproduced, stored in a retrieval system, or transmitted in any way by any means—electronic, mechanical, photocopy, recording, or otherwise—without the prior permission of the copyright holder, except as provided by USA copyright law.

Unless otherwise noted all scriptures are taken from the New American Standard Bible, © 1960, 1963, 1968, 1971, 1972, 1973, 1975, 1977 by The Lockman Foundation. Used by permission.

ISBN 1-57921-212-3
Library of Congress Catalog Card Number: 99-60373

The story you are about to read takes place several years in the future and is intended to be fictional. Any resemblance that the aliens mentioned herein may bear to actual beings from other planets is purely coincidental.

Contents

Prologue vii

Chapter 1:
    Welcome to My World 9
Chapter 2:
    I'm From the Government and I'm Here to Help 23
Chapter 3:
    Getting to Know You 35
Chapter 4:
    Stranger In a Strange Land 49
Chapter 5:
    In the Presence of My Enemies? 63
Chapter 6:
    Baby, It's a Wild World 79
Chapter 7:
    The Almighty Dollar 93

Chapter 8:
    The Dollar Rebounds 103
Chapter 9:
    The Good, the Greedy, and the Perverse 115
Chapter 10:
    The Cur Song 127
Chapter 11:
    I Love Me Just the Way I Am 135
Chapter 12:
    Deck Chairs on the Titanic 151
Chapter 13:
    All That Is In the World 171
Chapter 14:
    'Til Death Do Us Part 179

Epilogue 187

Prologue

The Curian fleet glided in silence past unfamiliar stars near the outer rim of the galaxy, their souls heavy with the knowledge that the unthinkable had occurred. One moment, they were all singing and laughing. Then, abruptly, one of their number experienced an *accident*—a concept which, until now, had been unknown to the Curians, as were these strange feelings of sadness and bewilderment.

Yet, they knew the risks. In fact, few races had dared to venture into this particular sector of the cosmos, but the Curians were insatiable explorers. Now one of their number was lost, and his friends could only speculate as to what might have become of their comrade.

Chapter 1

WELCOME TO MY WORLD

Dazed, but still conscious, the pilot and sole occupant of the Curian spacecraft struggled to take stock of his surroundings. He had suffered no physical harm, but remained as bewildered as the rest of the fleet by what had just taken place. The Curians have a long history of interstellar exploration and Curian technology is considered to be virtually flawless.

His vessel, which initially appeared as a dark, formless blotch to those few who saw it descend from the sky, came to a soft landing at a site selected automatically by its internal guidance systems. As it did so, the Curian pilot spoke out loud to himself—a practice common to many technologically advanced races. (Note: to assist the reader, the alien's comments have been roughly translated, where possible, into English as spoken in the late twentieth-century United

States). "Wow, what a rush! What just happened to me? I never felt anything like that before! And where am I?" He unbuckled his seat belt and, as his eyes began to clear, he stared in stunned disbelief at the readings on his panel of instruments.

Having concluded that they must have somehow suffered some kind of damage, the alien simply shrugged. *Oh well, might as well take a look outside.* He reached forward and cranked a handle several times. As he did so, a window gradually opened in the side of his ship, revealing an open field. *Hmmm, the central star of this planetary system is positioned low in the eastern sky. Looks like a pretty nice morning where I've landed. I wonder if those bipedal creatures staring in this direction are the dominant life-form here or if it's those four-legged guys. I guess I'll find out soon enough.*

He tapped his head twice. "Log entry, Curian universal memory, next available number, please." He grimaced. *Interesting, I'm not connecting, but I don't understand why.* He tapped a button on his control panel several times. "Log entry, Curian universal memory, next available number, please." Still no response.

He pressed another button. "Off-line log entry, Curian universal memory: I've been privileged to have a new and unique experience that I can not yet explain. While piloting a remote probe, I was forced to land on a life-bearing planet that I do not at all recognize. I've concluded that I should not have strayed so far from the rest of the fleet, but have not yet been able to formulate a logical explanation for my experience. Could it be that I've encountered some new cosmic phenomenon? I suppose that's possible. However, I'm more inclined to believe there's been some sort of systems malfunction. I cannot even determine where I am. Instrument readings make absolutely no sense.

"For example, from all appearances, the planet on which I've landed is composed entirely of standard B-type matter and supports carbon-based life. Nothing strange about that. However, readings indicate that spiritual activity is off the scale! There seems to be no reason why that should be the case, and yet my internal systems analysis continues to indicate that instrumentation is functioning according to design specifications. Therefore, either my vessel has malfunctioned in a manner previously unrecorded within the Curian universal memory, or I've landed on an extremely unusual world."

He placed the recorder on pause. "Well, I guess you live and learn." The tone of his voice changed as he chuckled lightly to himself. "All I ever hear is 'buy Curian, support local Curian contractors.' I'll be interested to hear what the boys in diagnostics have to say about this baby when I get home."

The Curian continued to examine his instruments and execute the standard procedures for initial contact with an alien world. "Off-line Curian universal memory log entry, resume: The language assimilator on this vessel also appears to be functioning normally, although there are many words and concepts within the indigenous speech for which there are no equivalents in my data banks. Perhaps the inhabitants of this world possess knowledge to which we have not yet been exposed."

He again placed his recorder on pause. "This is wild. In all the thousands of races we've encountered having cognitive thought processes and the ability to communicate, nothing like this has ever happened before. I can't wait to meet these people!"

Reactivating his recorder: "Have initiated reconfiguration of my ship to ensure stability in a B-type environment. As soon as I adapt my own molecular structure, I will attempt to communicate with the level one species here, wherever here is."

Although his craft had landed in a sparsely populated area, roughly two dozen onlookers had already arrived and were standing at a safe distance. As they watched, the formless blotch before them began to take shape. Abruptly, the alien vessel assumed the appearance of, for lack of any better description, a large brown box.

Preparations inside the vessel having been completed, the alien threw a rope ladder from the top of his "box" and began to descend. The onlookers backed away as the Curian came into view, even though his appearance was anything but threatening. He was roughly the same shade of brown as his ship, although his color seemed to shift almost imperceptibly at times. In most respects his form was almost human. He had two arms and two legs and stood erect, but his nose, if that's in fact what it was, was so large that the alien's head had the appearance of a misshapen watermelon. He had two small eyes, one on each side of his head, that were separated from each other by the huge nose and were similar in their positioning to those of a bird. His hair was combed neatly to the side.

The small group of people who stood watching trembled with anticipation, their imaginations running wild. Each recognized that he or she had suddenly and unexpectedly become part of an historic event of unparalleled significance. Some were filled with excitement and hope, some with fear, but none could have anticipated the events that were about to transpire.

As he descended, the alien smiled and waved. "Hi, how's it going? Nice day, huh?" He jumped the last several feet from his rope ladder and strode briskly towards the small group of native creatures. All but one of the onlookers, a young man in his twenties, quickly drew back. As the alien approached, he extended his hand to this one brave individual. "Cur, from the planet Curous, good to meet you."

The man was trembling, but somehow managed to sputter, "Ha...have you come in peace?"

The Curian was obviously puzzled by the question. "Yes, right, I come in peace. Now look, I hate to be a pest, but I'm wondering if you guys could help me out. Something happened to my vessel, and its internal guidance system brought me to your world, which, I might add, is quite beautiful, but I seem to be getting some ambiguous readings from my instruments. So, no offense, but could somebody start by telling me where I am."

He was met with silence, each of the onlookers apparently waiting for someone else to say something. Even the man who initially held his ground backed off. The alien waited for a minute or two, then thought to himself, *Maybe these creatures are not as intelligent as my shipboard monitors led me to believe. I'll try slowing down the pace of the dialogue.* "Me visitor from bright lights in sky, does this planet have name?"

By this time a few more people had arrived and a man wearing what the Curian later learned was a uniform stepped forward. "Sir, welcome to New Jersey." The alien, though encouraged by the response to his question, was still puzzled.

"This planet's named New Jersey? My instruments indicated I was supposed to land in a place called New Mexico, but that didn't make any sense either."

The man laughed nervously. "No, listen, actually this is Roswell, New Jersey." He coughed and cleared his throat. "The place you really want to be is a little south of here. If you're an alien, you want Washington D.C., where our government is. Now it's real easy to get to. All you need to do is to follow I-95, here, south for, oh I'd say about...."

He was cut short by another man who grabbed his arm and spun him around. The alien thought it strange that he was shouting in the first man's face. "Shut up you idiot! What if this creature's hostile? You want him to blow up the government?"

The first man pushed him away and shouted back. "I was hoping to just get him out of New Jersey. Let's let the Feds deal with whatever has to be dealt with here."

The alien meanwhile was smiling broadly. "Gentlemen, I appreciate greatly this show of concern for me, but all I really need to know for now is the name of your planet."

A young girl, clutching her father's hand called out, "Are you an angel?"

The alien laughed so loudly in response that all but the most courageous backed off a little further. "No honey, angels can get around without spaceships. Cute kid you have there, sir. Now please, somebody tell me where I am. For most level one species, this is not a tough question."

A man in the back shouted out, "This is Earth, buddy, and just for the record, we're well prepared to defend ourselves if you're thinking of trying anything funny!"

The Curian began to laugh again. "Hey pal, you're a real riot; everywhere I go I meet comedians, now come on, I've got a problem here, where am I really?"

The young girl who had asked whether the alien was an angel moved near the front of the crowd, which by this time had begun to grow. Still clutching her father's hand, she called out, "Mister, this really is Earth. You've landed on Earth."

The Curian's countenance changed very suddenly. He became somber and stared ahead in stunned silence for what seemed, to many of the onlookers, like an eternity. Several in the crowd, however, had begun to lose their initial inhibitions, most likely concluding that the visitor was not as threatening as they first feared. A young woman approached the alien with her arms stretched outward. "The child speaks the truth my friend." And then raising her voice she cried, "The people of Earth welcome you! Our world is your world. Let us learn from each other. Let us share one another's secrets. Let us savor the joys of peaceful...."

But her impassioned speech trailed off as she looked into the eyes of the Curian and saw only horror and disbelief. "This isn't a joke is it? You guys are really serious." The alien fell to his knees, lifted his eyes to the sky and cried, "Not Earth, O Lord, please not Earth! Is it so wrong to question? Of all the planets in the universe, why here?"

The crowd grew silent. Finally someone spoke. "Excuse me, but what's wrong with Earth?"

The Curian struggled to compose himself, "Because Earth is the only..." and then he stopped abruptly, as if some unseen presence had commanded him not to say any more.

Again came the question. "What's so bad about Earth?"

The alien started back towards his ship. "Uh, nothing, sorry to have bothered you folks. Now, if you'll excuse me, I've got to go somewhere and think."

The young woman who had begun the passionate speech called out after him. "Wait, don't leave, there is so much we can..."

But the alien held up his hand. "Relax, I'll be around," and turned again towards his ship.

But his first encounter with humankind was not to be so brief. The Curian had hardly taken two steps before he found himself covered with a net. Several men appeared who seemed determined not to let the visitor leave. Although their clothing differed, all wore some sort of numerical insignia that the alien could not quite make out. "Now don't get too close, boys," the leader shouted. "We don't know what kind of strange diseases this alien freak might be carrying, but he's much too big a prize to let get away."

The Curian appeared to be, in human terms, disgusted. "I refuse to believe this is happening to me. What is wrong with you people? Look, I just need a little time alone in my ship and I'll be back, I promise." But the visitor's attempts to reason with his captors were futile.

The leader of the group smiled. "Sorry Mr. Alien, we know you're upset, and I'm not sure yet what we're going to do with you, but you could be a once-in-a-lifetime opportunity to make some big money." The Curian's struggles and pleading appeared hopeless.

He felt himself being pushed through the rear doors of a van, and then, abruptly, a shot rang out. "Excuse me gentlemen, but this is a matter of national security." The crowd turned to see another man in uniform. "Now everybody listen very carefully. You did not see a UFO land here today; you did not speak with an alien visitor. Everybody got that?" He turned to the men holding the net. "Sorry boys, the alien's coming with me, don't make me get rough."

They dropped the net, but their leader shouted back, "You ain't heard the last of us (expletives deleted) soldier man. Whether you like it or not, this is going to be all over the six o'clock news."

The uniformed man said nothing, but escorted the Curian into his vehicle. As they began to drive off, he leaned over and whispered, "Is there some way you can move that thing you came in without actually going into it?"

The alien appeared to be insulted. "Of course."

"Then I suggest you move it to someplace where you won't have the whole world poking around it." The alien was about to ask why people on Earth would not respect someone else's property but, based upon what he had just been through, simply agreed. With hardly a sound, his cardboard box launched itself into orbit.

The man in uniform continued. "Actually, I'm taking a big chance here, but I'm guessing that you're too important to be left in the hands of those thugs. With any luck, there will be a few TV specials, and then the rest of the world will conclude that this never happened. We'll all be better off."

When they had gone a safe distance, the man began to unbutton his uniform. "How'd you like my little show back there?"

Once again the Curian was confused. "I don't get it, what are you talking about?"

The man laughed. "I retired from active duty years ago. I staged that little charade because I could see things getting out of hand. Somebody with a little common sense had to take control. You know, if any of those folks had taken the trouble to look at this contraption we're riding in, it would have been obvious it's not a military vehicle.

"Please don't ask me to explain, but for some reason I had the strongest feeling this morning that I ought to keep this uniform handy. Some people might say it was…well I don't know. Anyway, I'll bet that right about now the real military is combing the area. I'll leave it up to you whether you want them to find you or not, but like I said, we'll both be better off if they don't."

The alien was still confused. "Please go back over that again. This is all happening much too quickly. I may be a little slow sometimes, but I doubt that a even a Bonkarian elder could make sense of everything that's happened to me since I landed here."

His new friend laughed again. "A what? What is a Bonkarian elder? And remember, I've never been anywhere but Earth."

The Curian thought for a moment. "Well, basically the Bonkarians are a race of people who originate from the planet Bonkar. They're especially gifted thinkers, who spend a great deal of time in thought and meditation. Actually, we don't see them much, and it's difficult to get them to socialize. Now, please talk to me about what's going on here and explain why I might not want to be, uh, found."

The man sighed, "How do I explain this to somebody from outside our world? OK, if you stay in the area, it won't be long before they find you and when they do, they'll want to study you. They'll want to put you in custody, interrogate you, subject you to scientific tests, and worst of all might even demand that you fill out government forms and penalize you if you complete them incorrectly. As for me, I'll be in a whole lot of trouble for taking matters into my own hands and not turning you over to the authorities."

The alien stared at him quizzically. "Are you sure about that? Shouldn't the authorities be the people we want to see?"

"No, I'm not sure," the man replied quietly. "This is the first time I've ever rescued an alien from a gang of thugs. I'm not sure what I should be doing. I'm making it up as I go along."

The two rode in silence for several minutes. Finally the alien spoke again. "I still don't comprehend any of this, but thank you. I think I'm in your debt. But I've got to tell you something. Listen, please don't take offense at this, but in spite of all I've heard about Earth, I never expected the place to be so utterly bizarre. And another thing, why did all those people believe your fabrication, when it could so easily have been discovered?"

The man laughed loudly. "Lesson one about life on Earth, my extraterrestrial friend. You can say almost anything with a straight face and conviction in your voice and people will believe you. Now, how about you explaining something else. Just what did you mean by 'all you've heard about Earth'?"

The alien grimaced. "You know this is really awkward. Sometimes I say too much."

The man laughed again. "Look, what are you worried about? I'm the guy who should be worried. Here I am on a dark road with an alien in my truck. I've never even met an alien, let alone had one in my truck. Bottom line, I have no idea whether this pleasant conversation is going to continue or if you're going to shoot me, eat me, or take over my body. So whatever you've got to say, just spit it out. I won't be offended. And if you're here to conquer us, just do me a favor and go easy on me and my family."

The alien was speechless. Finally, he cleared his throat and stammered, "Well, you know, Curians do a lot of research, and, well you know, I might have picked up a little information about Earth along the way."

The man interrupted. "OK, you said Curians. I take it that's what you are. And you know something about Earth, and my guess from what you've said so far is that it's not very complimentary."

The alien found it curious that although the man was smiling his tone was so serious.

"Look, bottom line, I just pulled your alien back-side out of the fire, so I think I'm entitled to hear what you have to say."

Cur was silent for awhile and then suddenly burst into uproarious laughter. "Eat you? Take over your body? What are you talking about? From what I've heard about humans, I always assumed they could never possess a sense of humor, but you're a pretty funny guy. Admittedly, your humor is markedly different than that of the Curians, but I think I can get into it."

This time it was the human who was speechless. After almost a full minute of awkward silence, the alien continued.

"Did I say something wrong? All right, listen, I'm not supposed to even be on your planet. But now that I'm here, there are certain things about which I'm forbidden to speak. But I can tell you this, everybody in the universe knows about Earth."

That was too much for the man. He stopped the truck and stared at the alien. "Forbidden by whom?"

"Sorry, can't tell you."

"All right," the man shot back, "let's go back to 'everybody in the universe knows about Earth.' The universe is a pretty big place. Just what is it that everybody knows?"

"Sorry, can't tell you."

"Oh come on, give me something! I promise I won't be offended."

The alien hesitated, and then as if he were about to reveal some momentous secret replied softly, "All right, let me start by saying that when Curian children go camping, they like to sit around the fire and tell scary stories about Earth."

As the alien paused, the man stared in disbelief. Then he exploded, "That's it! That's it! OK, I get it. I know when I'm being had. I can take a joke. You got me. I'm on one of those hidden-camera TV shows, right? There's a camera hidden in that oversized schnozolla there, right?" He leaned over and took hold of the alien's head. "Unless I miss my guess, this thing should come right off."

The alien, meanwhile, was waving his arms in the air and shouting, "Help! Somebody please help! One of your fellow Earth people is hurting me."

That went on for four or five minutes. A number of other vehicles drove by, and several slowed to watch what appeared to be a man trying to get a watermelon off of the head of another man, but nobody stopped.

Finally, the man let go and muttered, "This is ridiculous," followed by something that the alien found to be incomprehensible. He started the truck again and the two rode on a little further in silence. Abruptly, the man extended his hand. "The name is Green, Bill Green, and yours?"

Cur flinched at first, thinking the man was about to grab his head again. He then cautiously extended his own hand and replied sheepishly, "Curians don't actually have names, but we suggest to species that do that they simply call us Cur."

Green grunted a kind of half laugh. "All right, I'll play along. So how do you function without names; how do you, oh, I don't know, call to someone in a crowd?"

"No problem. Just say something like, 'hey you in the plaid shorts,' and you don't need to be embarrassed if you can't remember the guy's name."

Green abruptly stopped the truck. "We'll pick this up later. Seems there is somebody else who needs my help."

A dog was wounded and lying on the side of the road, apparently struck by a car. "This is going to be tricky," Green grunted, "wounded animals can be dangerous."

Cur interjected, "Then let me get him, I'm not subject to the same risks of injury that you are."

Green was momentarily taken back and before he could make a move to stop him, Cur had the animal and, just as Green had feared, the dog sank his teeth into the alien's arm.

Cur cried out in pain, "Hey, that hurt!" and then gently lowered the dog into the back of the vehicle.

Green looked annoyed. "I thought you told me that nothing could happen to you."

It appeared as if the alien was crying. He was breathing heavily and his words came with difficulty. "I don't understand. Is this really what it's like? It's...it's terrible."

"So you can't be hurt, eh?"

Cur fought to regain his composure. "What I said was that there was no risk of injury or infection, at least there shouldn't be. I never said I wouldn't feel pain. But this is new to me. Pain never felt like this before."

Green was confused. "I still don't get it."

Cur began to explain, "Pain is a great teacher; everybody everywhere is subject to pain. The big difference on Earth, it seems, is that...is that..."

"Is what?" Green demanded.

"I'm sorry," Cur replied, "I guess sometimes I talk too much."

Green snorted, "And you say Earth is bizarre; I just hope I did the right thing rescuing you."

Cur forced a smile through the tears. "I have it on good authority that you did." The truck pulled into Green's driveway.

Chapter 2

I'm From the Government and I'm here to Help

Bill Green's wife, Mildred, met them at the door. "For crying out loud Bill, what have you drug home this time?"

"Listen Hon," he sighed, "what was I supposed to do, leave the poor dog in the road?"

"I don't mean the dog Bill, by now I'm used to the dogs. I mean that thing walking beside you on two legs."

Bill motioned matter-of-factly towards the alien. "Oh, sorry...Mildred meet Cur. Cur, this is my wife, Mildred."

Mildred started to chuckle, "Who is this guy, Bill? Is this some relative you didn't want me to know about until after we got married and had kids?"

Bill replied sheepishly, "Look Hon, Cur's a, uh, an alien, you know, like on TV, except he's a nice alien, I think. Right, Cur?"

Mildred was leaning against the door with her arms folded. "So what you're telling me is, tonight you brought home a Martian."

"Now look Hon, I know this is hard to believe, but this guy's not from Earth. Cur is a Curian from the planet Curous."

Mildred turned to the alien. "I have an aunt who lives in Curous. Moved there from Hoboken. Now, is Cur your first name or last name?"

"Well, actually, everybody from my planet is named Cur."

Bill interrupted. "Listen Millie, Cur is hurt, the dog bit him, would you mind looking at his arm?"

The alien held out his arm. "What was your name again? Oh yeah, Bill, look, I'm OK, the healing process has already begun. I just need a little energy to get my strength back."

Mildred gestured towards the kitchen, "Then come in and join us for dinner."

As Mildred began to set another place at the table, Cur took Bill's arm. "Listen, there's something else I have to tell you about Curians. We don't ingest material food."

Bill asked the obvious question, "How, then, do you live?"

"We absorb energy directly from our environment, so I really can't eat with you, as much as I appreciate the hospitality, but it would be great if you could let me stand next to that thing for a while with the door open." He pointed to the oven.

Green was about to attempt an explanation to his wife, but she had overheard. "Go ahead, what's your name, uh . . .

Cur, it's the least we can do for someone who looks as bad as you do, by human standards of course." Then she turned to Bill, "You know, this is going to be brutal on a summer night; where do you dig up these people?"

Strangely enough, the temperature in the kitchen did not rise. In fact, there was an unusual chill in the air, and Cur seemed refreshed and strengthened.

After dinner Bill and Mildred started putting dishes in the sink and noticed that Cur had left the kitchen and was looking around in the living room. Mildred was a little concerned that this stranger should be left to wander through their house unattended, and so Bill went out after him.

He found the alien studying several pictures on a mantel above the fireplace. Cur picked one up. "Who are these people?"

"Those are my parents."

Cur stared at the picture for a moment. "Why do they appear to be so wrinkled?"

Bill laughed, "That happens to Earth people as they age." He could have been mistaken, but he thought he saw the alien shudder.

Cur picked up another picture.

Bill pointed to a woman in the center. "That's Sara, my daughter, with her husband, Rob, and their children. Do Curians have families?"

The alien began to say something, but somehow could not get out the words. Bill suddenly felt extremely awkward, as it appeared that the alien was about to become emotional. While trying to think of something to say next, he was mercifully rescued by his wife.

She called from the kitchen, "Hey Mr. Space-age Good Samaritan, I think you and your pal made the news."

The television was on in the other room, and Cur found it fascinating. "What is this, some sort of communications device?"

Bill laughed, "It's a one-way communications device. It speaks, we listen. Some people think it's a source of a lot of trouble in this world."

Cur appeared confused. "Then why do you have one in your home?"

Bill thought for a moment. "Let me put it this way, it's like anything else, you have to control it. If it controls you, then it becomes dangerous."

Mildred smiled wryly. "I just learned something tonight. When the hockey game's on, you're controlling the TV. The TV's not controlling you. That's good to know."

They had no way of suspecting just how ironic this conversation would someday prove to be. For the moment however, their attention was drawn to the flickering light before them and the media account of the day's events.

The alien leaned forward in his chair, intrigued by what was before him. Following several short clips of Earth people engaged in various activities, accompanied by music which the alien found emotionally stirring, three people appeared behind a long desk. Abruptly however, only the man seated in the middle was visible. The music stopped, and the man began to speak.

"Good evening, the area is buzzing today with stories of a strange alien spacecraft that allegedly landed not far from here and then left again, but without its occupant, who is rumored to be still at large." Cur turned to Bill and Mildred, smiled and pointed to himself.

"While the accounts differ, most have the alien saying something like, 'Oh Lord, why here,' presumably addressing what some religious groups refer to as God. Following a rehash of the stories we brought you last evening, the weather and a few jokes, we'll have interviews with a number of people who claim to have been present at what may be mankind's first face-to-face encounter with a being from another world."

Bill sighed, "Well Cur, I'm sure you'll want to see this, but we have to wait about a half-hour. Do Curians play cards?"

Cur, however, was still mesmerized by the screen. "Bill, what is this? What's this woman talking about so sincerely? Apparently it's a matter of serious concern to human women."

Bill cleared his throat. "That's called a commercial, and the woman is talking about, about, uh, hey Millie, do me a favor and explain this to our friend."

Millie walked over chuckling as she dried a dish. "Listen Mr. Hotshot. You're this guy's friend, you explain it."

Bill mumbled, "Remind me Cur, I'll tell you about it later."

They eventually made it through the rest of the news, with Cur asking quite a few questions and Bill saying, "Please, I'm trying to hear this," or some variation thereof. At last, they heard the anchorman say, "UFO mania refuses to die down, and I have some people here who claim to have actually had an encounter with an extraterrestrial being in South Jersey this morning. Sir, can you tell me what you saw and what happened?"

The leader of the group wearing the numerical insignias stepped forward. Bill Green leaned over and whispered, "Hey Cur, you remember this guy?"

"Well, me and the boys were trying to help the spaceman, but he threatened to infect us with killer space germs, so we had to back off. I say we find that thing and kill it before it comes after our wives and kids."

Cur exploded, "Nothing he said was even close to the truth! What's with that guy? Don't people on Earth have any regard for the truth?"

Mildred broke in, "It's a long story. Can we talk about it during a commercial?"

The camera focused on a woman who was obviously stricken with panic. "He was hideous, with flashing green eyes and saliva dripping from his mouth. The gentleman was right, this thing must be killed!"

"Just for the record," Cur muttered, "Curians don't even have saliva glands."

Now the camera was on the young woman who first welcomed Cur to Earth. "No, no, it wasn't like that at all! He spoke eloquently and with passion about the need for all people and animals everywhere to become one with the cosmic vibrations that can heal our world, restore good feelings, and bring peace to our cities. It's time for people all over the world to...."

Mercifully, the newscaster broke in, "Excuse me, but we have time for just one more."

A stern-faced, elderly gentleman stepped forward. "Don't you people get it, this is nothing but an advertising gimmick. The New Jersey Department of Agriculture is trying to get people to buy watermelons."

After what seemed like an interminable silence, Cur said softly, "This is wild. I've personally traveled to hundreds of planetary systems in this region of the galaxy, and other Curians have been to many thousands more, but I've experienced things today that have no parallel to anything anywhere in the Curian collective memory. I know I'm your guest here and I certainly don't wish to cause offense, but how does anyone go about his or her business day to day on such a bizarre world?"

Bill smiled broadly. "Welcome to Earth."

Mildred appeared to be in shock. "Bill, I just realized. I . . . I thought this was another one of your jokes! But those people did see something, and you really did bring a man from another planet into our home."

A huge smile still in place, he replied, "Yes, dear."

Needless to say, nobody slept that night. Both the Earth people and the Curian seemed to have an insatiable appetite to learn from the other. Bill and Mildred, for their part, grew a little tired of hearing, "Sorry, I can't discuss that," but kept a tape-recorder running hoping to glean whatever information they could from this strange visitor. Cur employed his own recording device. By the time Bill and Mildred realized how long they had been talking, the sun had risen.

As morning broke, there was a knock at the door. "Open up, this is the government."

Bill walked towards the door, took hold of the knob and hesitated. "Could you be a little more specific?" he asked dryly. Silence. "Let me try again," Bill continued, "which department or agency of the government? Are you federal, state, or local? Because I want to see some ID and hear a good explanation for this before I open the door."

Again silence, and then a voice answered with unaccustomed meekness, "The alien being who landed in New Jersey yesterday was traced to your house, but we couldn't decide who had jurisdiction, so everybody came."

Mildred looked blankly at her husband. "You think I should put on another pot of coffee?"

Bill opened the door a crack. Before him were assembled, as far as the eye could see, a multitude of representatives from thousands of government agencies.

"Listen," he whispered to those closest to the door, "get out while you still can. There's an orbiting spacecraft out there that has enough firepower to reduce this planet to a cinder. This creature is extremely dangerous, you don't want to make it angry."

Cur moved towards the door and tapped Green's shoulder. "Excuse me Bill, I don't mean to interrupt, but I don't possess anything harmful to...."

Green spun towards Cur, hoping that those outside had not heard him. "Would you please shut up, I'm trying to help you."

But Cur gently brushed him aside and went outside to face the crowd. "I appreciate what you're doing, Bill, but like it or not, the fact is I'm here and I'm ready to face the implications of being here. Whatever happens to me on this, pardon the expression, insane world, I will always treasure your and Mildred's friendship. Stay in touch."

Then turning to the throng of public servants before him, he said: "People of Earth, I submit to your judgment regarding my fate. As far as I am permitted, I will open to you the wonders of the universe. I ask only three things in return, a power source, access to your libraries, and a trombone."

The crowd became tense and uneasy. Finally someone spoke, "We'll have to take this up with our superiors. The power source and the libraries should not be a problem, but no one seems to have a trombone in their budget. We can assure you, however, it's being looked into."

Someone from one of the environmental agencies approached with what looked like an astronaut's suit. "Here, put this on," he said firmly.

Cur responded, "Look, I know I don't exactly match, you know how it is in the morning when you're in a hurry, but this just isn't me." The man's expression never changed.

He entered the house with two more suits. "Good morning Mr. and Ms. Green, put these on."

Mildred started to object, "Wait just a second young man, this is America, who do you think...?"

He glared at her. "Put it on voluntarily, or we will force you into it. You and your husband are to be quarantined along with the extraterrestrial. You have been in his presence too long. We will not risk the spread of alien infection."

Cur, who had reentered the house in the commotion, approached Bill and Mildred. "What's his problem?"

Bill shrugged. "I guess he's just a conscientious guy who's been watching too many UFO specials on television. Under normal circumstances, he's probably a likable fellow."

Mildred snarled, "Bill, you're such a goody-goody, you're driving me nuts. For once, just say something nasty and get it out of your system!"

Bill went on, "Just keep in mind, Cur, what you said about valuing our friendship, because we're liable to be cooped up together for a long time."

The three were led away and ushered into the back of a truck, where they were held under armed guard, still not knowing their destination.

For a time no one said anything. Then Cur broke the silence. Turning to one of the guards, he asked, "Excuse me sir, but how long do you think it will be before I get my trombone? You know, throughout the cosmos there are few things that produce as sweet a sound as a trombone. I'm actually surprised you have them on Earth."

The guard remained expressionless.

Cur turned to Bill and Mildred, "I just thought a little conversation would make the ride go faster."

After what seemed like an interminable silence, Cur spoke again, "Excuse me sir, I don't mean to complain, but I'm having a problem with this suit, I really need to get out of it."

The guard shrugged, "Sorry buddy, I've got my orders."

Mildred took hold of Bill's arm. "Hey, I don't think Cur looks so good."

It was true. Cur was beginning to slump in his seat and his face, so far as they could tell, looked awful. Bill reached over and shook the Curian, then jumped up and screamed, "Energy, he needs energy and he can't get enough through that insulated suit. Listen to me, you've got to get him out of that suit and out of the back of this truck. He might die!"

The guard shot back, "Better him than the whole human race. You heard what the scientist said back there."

Bill was still on his feet. "That was no scientist. He was a political appointee, and there are no alien measles to wipe us out. For crying out loud, Cur's not even made of the same kind of matter we are."

The truck stopped abruptly and Bill fell forward. The driver's voice came across an intercom. "Everybody relax. It seems someone left an awfully big refrigerator box in the middle of the road. We'll have it moved in a second."

But the "box" was not to be moved. Instead, a voice emanated from within. "This unit is engaged in the preservation of sentient life. Please disembark from your vehicle."

The message was repeated three times, but those in the truck had been told to hold their ground. Suddenly, an energy beam flashed from the box and focused on the truck, and again, a voice emanated from the alien public address system. "The temperature of your vehicle will rise to a point of discomfort but not damage. It is recommended that you disembark."

Finally, somebody yelled, "All right, get the extraterrestrial out of there!"

Once he was outside, another beam from the box pierced Cur's quarantine suit and he began to revive.

Bill and Mildred ran to him. "We thought you were going to die," Mildred cried.

Cur looked thoughtful for a moment and then replied, "You know, that might be a possibility. I can't believe I didn't think of it until now. Having been on Earth and exposed to…uh, you know, conditions here, I guess it's possible."

Cur removed the suit and started towards his ship. Motioning with his hands, he addressed a stunned audience. "Listen my Earthling friends, I'm not one to be a party-pooper, but this is just not working. Please let me get back to my ship. I'll schedule a press conference sometime tomorrow and do my best to answer all of your questions."

Several of the guards raised their weapons, but their commanding officer shouted, "Don't shoot the alien."

One asked, "But why, sir?"

With impatience in his voice, he grunted, "Because everybody knows it's always wrong to shoot the alien. Either it won't hurt him, or something terrible will happen to us, or both."

Cur chuckled to himself and decided that he would not correct his benefactor. After all, getting shot would hurt. This time, he made it to his ship, climbed the rope ladder to get inside, and in an instant his vessel disappeared into the sky.

Chapter 3

GETTING TO KNOW YOU

IT WAS A WEEKNIGHT and millions of television aficionados across the country were actively engaged in their sitcom of choice, blissfully unaware that their planned viewing was about to be interrupted by a public announcement of historical significance. Without warning, an alien face flashed abruptly onto millions of TV screens, interrupting the regularly scheduled programming of both national and local networks. "Hi, people of Earth. Sorry for the intrusion, but I've been advised that this is the most efficient way to communicate with a large percentage of the human population." He smiled broadly as he spoke. Many viewers thought they heard trombones playing in the background.

"I'm a Curian from the planet Curous. You can call me Cur. I'm speaking to you tonight from my spacecraft, which at this moment is orbiting your planet. Uh, let me see here a minute. Well, if you have a good pair of binoculars, you can probably see me from the eastern half of Australia. I'll turn on the outside lights."

Across the United States, people of all ages and backgrounds were attempting frantically to change channels, in the desperate hope of finding something more familiar, but to no avail. The Curian broadcast continued on all stations.

"You may have heard how I landed on your planet the day before yesterday. Well, I feel badly about getting so many people upset, so I thought I should give you a chance to have your questions answered. From what I can tell, you folks have some pretty wild ideas about people like me who come from other planets, so I hope to be able to clear up a few misconceptions. I'll be holding a press conference in the courtyard of the State House Annex next to the Capitol Building in Trenton, New Jersey tomorrow morning at 10:00 A.M. That will give those of you who work in the area, and may not be especially interested in what I have to say, a chance to get to work before the streets become congested.

"Oh, and before I forget, if the governor of New Jersey is watching, listen, you probably ought to get somebody to look at your telephone system. I tried several times to make arrangements for this through your office, but somehow kept getting cut off.

"Sorry about the short notice, but I'm trying to make things easier on a couple of friends of mine. Anyway, I won't need any special equipment; I can bring my own amplification system. Everybody's invited. I'd love to see you. Now I, uh...return you to your regularly scheduled programming. Bye." Instantly the image was gone, and the usual programs returned.

Not surprisingly, the networks were flooded with calls, although reactions to the unexpected announcement varied greatly. Some callers expressed anger because they missed the ends of their shows, but most wanted more information. Many of the sponsors, whose commercials were overridden, were enraged, demanding refunds of their advertising dollars. The stations themselves, of course, had no explanation for what had happened. Interestingly, many viewers were not even aware that anything unusual had taken place until it was reported on the news later that evening.

As might be imagined, not all calls were made to the television networks. Phone lines were jammed with calls to the police and elected officials, who were subjected to a relentless chorus of, "The Earth is in trouble and it's your job to take care of us." Foreign governments were demanding to know why they had not received formal invitations to the first news conference with an extraterrestrial visitor. UFO sightings were at record highs all over the world that night, but especially in Australia.

And while a world in turmoil tried to prepare, as well as it could, for its first verifiable meeting with an extraterrestrial, Cur himself spent the rest of the night relaxing with a few books he had borrowed from the Greens, eventually falling into a sound sleep.

The following morning, Trenton, New Jersey found itself the center of worldwide attention. The city was in chaos. Thousands fled, convinced that alien invaders had selected Trenton to be the focal point of their attack on Earth. Thousands more entered the city and spent the night camped as closely as possible to the State House Annex, anxious to be among the first humans to meet the strange visitor. Among them were journalists from all over the globe, dreaming of an opportunity to be part of something that would forever change the course of human history. Although many in

Washington, D. C. remained convinced that the alien broadcast was only a hoax, the National Guard was still much in evidence, if only to keep order.

Vendors had set up souvenir stands on almost every street corner. Many had life-size cardboard Curians with which visitors to Trenton could have their pictures taken.

At precisely 10:00 A.M., EST, the Curian spacecraft descended from the sky, hovered above State Street in Trenton and then moved silently towards its designated landing area. The crowd went wild and quickly became a mob as many tried to elbow their way to a more advantageous position. Attorneys in the group began to take names and distribute business cards, hoping to bring suit against the planet Curous for any injuries that might result.

Above the din, a clear, commanding voice rang out, "Excuse me, but would somebody mind clearing a spot for me to stand? Excuse me, uh, if you people keep pushing and hurting each other, then I'll uh, I'll uh, let me see, I'll be forced to do something, you know, of a less than optimal nature." Several people in uniform were attempting to clear the landing area but with little success.

Again, a commanding alien voice cut through the commotion. "Oh come on people, get a grip! Look, I'm coming down, you better get out of the way." The ship descended slightly. "See, I'm serious, I'm really doing this, you better get out of the way, because I'm really coming down. You better get out of the way." The ship descended a little more.

Finally, after almost two hours, the crowd began to settle down and a space was cleared for the alien. His ship hovering several feet above the landing site, Cur descended his now familiar rope ladder with some sort of pouch strung around his shoulder. He was wearing a tee shirt which read, "Trenton Makes, the World Takes."

With the spacecraft continuing to hover silently overhead, Cur removed a small object from his pouch and placed it on the ground. As he lifted his head, he smiled and held up one finger. "Excuse me ladies and gentlemen, this will just take a second." He reached up, pulled something that looked like a garden hose from the bottom of his ship, turned the nozzle and squirted the object. As he did so, the object grew in size and took the shape of a speaking platform.

The alien again turned to his audience, smiling. "Pretty neat, huh?" He lifted a portable microphone from the pouch and began to unfold it. He tapped on it, and drawing it very close, he said in a low voice, "Testing, testing; can you people in the back hear me? Wave your hands if you can hear me. OK, great."

Aside from a few obligatory coughs, the crowd grew silent.

"It's a real privilege for me to be here in Trenton this morning and to share this time with you. I'm sure you folks are all very busy, and I want you to know how much I appreciate your making the effort to be here. I'll try not to take too much of your time. You know, back on Curous, I'm considered a pretty good story teller, and so I'd like to begin with a humorous anecdote that I often use in first contact situations with alien cultures."

Bill and Mildred Green, meanwhile, who were still in isolation but watching the broadcast from their containment room, groaned in unison, "Do we have to listen to this again?"

Not hearing them, of course, Cur went on, "It seems there were these three sentient life-forms in a boat, a muetoid, a buetoid, and a zarf. The zarf said, 'I have to go to the bathroom,' and he walked across the surface of the water to shore and then returned. The buetoid expressed a similar need, and he also walked across the surface of the water to shore and back again. The muetoid thought to himself, *if these guys can do it, so can I.* He got out of the boat and promptly sank. As the muetoid pulled himself back into the boat, the buetoid said to the zarf, 'Do you think we should tell him that buetoids and zarfs are composed of massless particles?'"

For a moment, there was silence, followed by some polite laughter. Many in the audience began to leave.

"All right, I can see I'm dying up here. You guys are almost as tough an audience as the Frumpians. But do you get the point? Your fears about me are as insubstantial as the buetoid and the zarf. Now I can't help but notice there are quite a few people from the press who were kind enough to be here, so why don't I open this up for questions. OK, you sir, go ahead."

A man in the crowd was given a microphone. "Mr. Cur, this question relates to your opening remarks. Maybe I'm missing something, but it doesn't seem logical that massless beings could relieve themselves of bodily fluids, because the fluids themselves would have mass."

Cur put his hand on his head, sighed and then responded. "Don't you get it? That's one of many inconsistencies that make the story so funny. Sorry, but based on my initial contact with your race, I assumed Earth people were created with a better sense of humor. Sorry, my mistake. Next question please."

Cur motioned to a woman, who quickly received a microphone. "Let me first say that Earth people do have a sense of humor, and I for one thought your story was great. My question is can you tell us where you're from? Where exactly is Curous?"

Cur scratched his head. "Hmmm, I knew I should have brought a map with me. Well, let me see. Let's say that this woman over here with the bad hair is the double star you call Beta Cygnus, and that fellow there wearing the headphones is Gamma Sagitta. Draw a straight line from where I'm standing to a point between the apparent positions of those two and follow it about 1,200 light years to somewhere around that bald guy in the back. When you see the Dumbbell Nebula coming up on your left, make a right. You can't miss it."

The cameras focused on another gentleman. "Do you have any special powers that we don't have; for example, are you physically stronger than us, can you read minds, can you change shape?"

Cur appeared perplexed. "Not really. You realize, of course, that this world was designed for you and the lifeforms in your care. It's highly doubtful that someone from the outside, compatible with a totally different environment would have abilities here that you don't have. No offense, but that just doesn't make sense. As a matter of fact, I would not be able to exist here at all if I had not adjusted my molecular structure, and that of my ship."

A woman had the next question. "Sir, if I might pick up on your last answer, some of the people who saw you first land said that your ship initially had an indefinite shape and no color. Shape and color were assumed after landing. Can you explain that, and can you tell us what kind of material you are made of?"

Cur thought for a moment and said. "This is going to be difficult to explain without getting too technical, but let me try. During the early years of our scientific endeavors, one of the things that drove the Curians absolutely bananas concerned the amount of matter in the universe.

Our calculations of observable gravitational effects seemed to indicate that a large portion of the matter in the universe was somehow missing. That, of course, did not make sense. It was centuries, however, before we discovered alternative forms of matter, which are not made up of the familiar protons, neutrons, and electrons and so exhibit radically different properties. The most prominent among those forms of alternative matter is that which we now refer to as 'type A'. My vessel is composed largely of type A matter. That is why, as I've already mentioned, in order to be stable in this environment, I had to…"

Suddenly, without warning, another commanding voice was heard, "Cut, commercial break, everybody take five."

Cur objected, "Wait a minute! I'm not done yet."

A man holding a clipboard emerged from the crowd. "Don't worry pal, you'll be back on in a minute. And a word of advice, keep your answers short, the American people have a very brief attention span. If cosmic phenomena can't be explained in a few sentences, the public doesn't want to hear about it. Keep up the technical mumbo-jumbo and you'll bore them to tears."

Cur swallowed his irritation. "I'm a guest on your world, and good manners would dictate that I honor your wishes. I'm sure you would not have interrupted me if these commercial messages were not critically important."

Someone handed the alien a battery-powered TV, and he gazed in bewilderment at a contest between beer bottles.

Learning firsthand that waiting through short commercial breaks can seem like an eternity, Cur was finally given the signal. He asked for another question.

Another man took the microphone. "Do Curians come in different sexes, and, if so, is there a special someone waiting for you out there?"

Cur appeared visibly shaken and his voice lost that lighthearted quality that prevailed earlier. "Yes, Curians were created male and female, just like you; and yes, I have a wife. She's a wonderful woman, quiet and shy, like a delicate flower. You cannot imagine the pain I feel in my soul knowing that I will most likely never see her again."

His answer had practically every member of the press corps clamoring for attention. Another woman was recognized, and she breathlessly grabbed the microphone. "You keep saying things like 'created' and 'designed.' Is it possible that a being like you, obviously part of a technologically advanced civilization, doesn't understand how the universe actually came into being? Maybe we've hit on something you can learn from us. Is it possible you actually believe in the existence of a Creator?"

Cur's countenance began to lighten and the familiar grin returned. "Thank you. That was great. I needed that. Nowhere else in the entire universe would anyone remotely consider asking a question like that. I was right about humans, you do have a sense of humor!"

From the same woman, "All right then, a follow-up question. Tell us about God." When she said, "God," Cur thought he detected a tone of contempt. Surely he must have been mistaken.

The woman continued. "I'm not laughing. You could be in a lot of trouble. This isn't the twentieth-century."

Cur gradually became serious again. What could she have meant? "Actually, there's not much I can tell you about God, but it doesn't matter. You already have all the information you need. And if you don't believe it now, nothing I say will convince you."

The mike was passed to someone else. "You said you may never see your wife again. Why?"

Once again Cur had to fight to maintain his composure. "Because I can never leave Earth, and she probably has no idea that anything happened. You know, we're not one of those couples that normally volunteer for separate missions, but the Curian fleet encountered an anomaly in the vicinity of the Pleiades and needed someone with her expertise to participate in the analysis. It wasn't really on the way, but, hey, we figured we'd eventually rendezvous in this sector. Anyway, even if she did manage to find me, my love for her would never let me ask her to join me here."

He paused and seemed to momentarily relax. "You know, she's very bashful, hardly says a word." He laughed lightly. "Nothing like me."

More follow-up questions ensued. "Why can't you leave? Won't the Curians have rescue teams looking for you? And what's so bad about Earth that you wouldn't bring your wife here?"

Cur was still shaken. "Please, there is very little I am permitted to say about those matters. Can we go on to another topic, OK, you sir, with the beard."

Several in the crowd shouted, "Permitted by whom?"

The cameras focused on a rather large, rough looking man. "Are there other intelligent alien races out there, or are you it?"

"No," Cur answered. "Actually, the Curians have encountered thousands of what we refer to as 'level one' races, or those having significant cognitive abilities, including symbolic thinking and abstract reasoning. Many of those species are actively exploring the cosmos, as we are."

The man wasn't finished. "Then would you mind telling the world, which of those species is kidnapping humans, performing experiments on them, and then returning them with their memories erased? I'm willing to bet that it's your lot and that this whole interview is nothing but a big cover-up!"

Cur was speechless. Fortunately, it was time for another commercial break. Unfortunately, many people had left to do something productive while the commercials were being aired and did not make it back in time to hear Cur's response. A seed had been planted in the public consciousness that would soon begin to take root.

When Cur was back on the air, he did his best to disavow any knowledge regarding alien abduction of humans. He went on to explain that occasionally the Zurkidians have been known to dispatch unmanned probes to fly by and film the natural beauty of the planet, but there was never any actual contact. Cur concluded, "No offense sir, but your question is preposterous. There is no reason anyone would want to do as you suggest." However, it was evident that the damage had been done.

Cur was beginning to get that "need for energy" look again and called for a final question.

A petite young woman asked, "Did I hear you say that all Curians are named Cur?"

Cur smiled. "We get that question a lot. Most of the intelligent races we've encountered utilize individual names, as you do on Earth, and as we did at one time. However, on Curous we decided that names were more trouble than they were worth. Curians for some reason have a terrible time remembering names. People kept forgetting them, and that led to all kinds of awkward social situations and misunderstandings. So now, if we want someone's attention, we just say something like, 'Hey, you in the blue shirt.' It's much more efficient than trying to remember names."

But that was not to be the last question. When he got to "Hey, you in the blue shirt," the bearded man with the question about alien abductions, pushing other people aside, ran to the woman holding the microphone. He grabbed the mike and shouted, "You're a liar pal, and I can prove it!"

Many in the crowd gasped, and the man continued, "You said earlier that your type of matter doesn't show color the way ours does, right? And yet you just used an example of one Curian saying to another, 'Hey you in the *blue* shirt.'" Then he turned to the crowd and shouted, "Let's show this creep how we handle aliens who do weird things to humans!"

While Cur tried to explain the misunderstanding, the man pushed through the crowd to where the alien was standing and, before the authorities could stop him, began swinging his fists wildly, shouting, "Welcome to Earth!" Cur, not knowing quite what to make of this, and assuming that the man's behavior represented some sort of ceremonial greeting, began to dance around and imitate the man's movements the best he could. Abruptly, the man's fist connected with the alien's midsection. As Cur doubled over in pain, the man's other fist came up on the alien's nose.

Cur fell backwards to the ground and a mechanical voice emanated from the spacecraft, which was still hovering above. "There is danger of injury to a sentient *life-form*. Prepare for intervention by this unit."

The man felt himself being separated from the alien, pushed back by some unseen force.

Cur, meanwhile, had gotten back on his feet and watched with a puzzled expression as the man was taken away by the police. He looked out on the crowd and asked, "Would somebody please explain what happened? I confess that I'm unfamiliar with Earth customs. Why would that gentleman, in the midst of an exchange of ideas, suddenly shout 'welcome to Earth' and then strike me in such a way as to cause pain? That is a form of greeting that I've not yet encountered."

No answer was forthcoming, however, as the crowd had erupted into a state of chaos. Cur quietly climbed his rope ladder and, once inside, piloted his ship to a point several miles above the surface. Possibly a careful review of the ship's tapes of his first public appearance before humanity would shed some light on the experience. He concluded that he really needed to learn more about this species before again attempting public contact.

Chapter 4

STRANGER IN A STRANGE LAND

THE GREENS HAD BEEN TAKEN to a secured military facility where they were placed in isolation and questioned extensively regarding their experiences with the alien visitor. They were also subjected to a battery of tests. No unusual physical problems or conditions were detected, but psychological tests revealed that Mildred harbored an unhealthy aversion to hamsters. After two weeks, they were both released on the condition that Mildred receive counseling.

Bill and Mildred also found themselves besieged with lucrative offers from publishers, filmmakers, and theme parks, as well as both day and late-night talk shows. As graciously as they could, they took those under advisement. Cur was clearly a hot item, and by virtue of the time spent with him, so were they.

They just could not shake the feeling, however, that there was something wrong with cashing in on a friendship—even friendship with an alien—and so they prayed about it and waited to see if Cur would return. (Note: The inclusion in the narrative of this action by the Greens should not be construed as an attempt to impose religious beliefs on others.)

Finally one night, the phone rang. It was Cur.

Bill was ecstatic at first, then cautious. "Wait a minute, you may sound like Cur, but then, we've been receiving a lot of crank calls here lately, how do I know it's you?"

There was silence for a moment. Then Mildred poked her husband. "Why don't you ask him something only Cur would know?"

Bill nodded his agreement. "Right, OK, I've got it. If you're really Cur, answer this question. Why did the chicken cross the galactic divide?"

The voice on the other side was quick to respond. "In order to verify Bonkarian calculations regarding the extent of temporal distortions."

With that, both Bill and the caller burst into laughter. Mildred, meanwhile, remained expressionless. "All right, it's him."

Bill held the phone aside and gestured to his wife, "C'mon Honey, don't you get it?" and then back to Cur, "Don't feel bad, I'm still trying to get her to appreciate British humor too."

Mildred picked up another phone. "All I can say is, that's got to be the worst joke I've ever heard. Nobody would think it was funny except my husband and an alien. Now, Cur, if you don't mind, it's science fiction week on our local station, and I'm trying to learn the truth about you guys."

Cur cleared his throat. "Well in that case, you'd better look at your TV."

As Bill and Mildred turned to look, Cur appeared on the screen. "We interrupt this deodorant commercial to bring you something far less sexy and informative."

Bill burst into laughter again. Mildred said simply, "You realize, of course, you're destroying all I've ever learned at the movies."

The conversation continued to be light hearted for the next few minutes, but the alien was hurting. It soon became apparent that he had begun to master the human art of covering pain with levity.

The fact of the matter was that Cur desperately needed someone to help him sort things out, but more than that, he was starving for a little personal contact with someone he could trust. He wanted to see his human friends, but the Greens suggested that it might not be a good idea for him to come to their home. The area was, of course, being watched closely by the FBI and local police, although that was not their primary concern. They would always be under surveillance by the authorities. The Greens, however, really hoped to keep their alien friend from the thousands of snoopers and curiosity-seekers that seemed to lurk behind every tree.

Finally, Mildred suggested that they meet in New York City. Cur was puzzled. "As usual, I'm missing something. Isn't New York one of the most heavily populated areas on Earth? Why New York?"

"Because," Mildred explained, "you won't be noticed in New York. It's a well known fact that no matter what you look like or what's happening to you, nobody pays any attention. The place is perfect."

It was agreed, and a few days later they met on the designated corner. Bill and Mildred were right. As Cur's ship descended into Manhattan, nobody even looked up. In fact, the only people to notice were tourists on the top of the Empire State Building who, it might be noted, managed to get some great photographs of family members posing in front of the alien space craft.

Once they were together, Bill and Mildred hugged their alien friend. Cur was smiling broadly. "Finally, a form of greeting with which I'm familiar. You know, given conditions here, there really ought to be a lot more hugging going on."

Bill was smiling also, but was visibly nervous. "Good to see you, but honestly Cur, I don't really think the hat and trench coat are going to hide who you are. Besides, we're followed everywhere we go. In fact, there's no question that we're being watched at this moment."

Cur's face twisted into a look of perplexity "Again, I don't get it. Why doesn't whoever is watching us just walk over and do whatever it is they're going to do?"

"Because," replied Bill, "the incidents with the heat-ray and force-beam have the authorities a little rattled. They're afraid to try to take you by force against your will, and so for now, they're content to monitor your movements and ours."

He took Cur by the arm. "Let's sit down in that coffee shop across the street."

As they tried to enter the little restaurant, they were abruptly stopped at the door. A large man in a beat-up T-shirt and a shabby chef's hat growled, "Excuse me buddy, but didn't you see da sign?"

Cur turned to read, "No Curians Allowed."

The man went on. "Look pal, you gotta understand, it's nothin' poisonal."

"Nothing personal?" Cur shouted. "How could it not be personal? I'm the only Curian on the planet!"

"See," said Mildred, "I told you we wouldn't be noticed."

Bill countered, "I guess the guy is new in town."

Mildred agreed. "His accent needs work. Come on, we've rented a motel room. Let's just go there."

Motel employees are, of course, trained to be polite and professional to all their clients. However, noting the stares, Bill still found it necessary to lean over the counter and whisper, "He was dropped on his head several times as an infant."

Cur, for his part, was utterly fascinated by the newsstand in the lobby. While Bill was checking in, he called to Mildred, "Would you please buy me some of these?"

"Certainly," replied Mildred. "I can't think of any better way to integrate you into our culture."

Cur's face wore its now customary look of incomprehension. "After a few brief encounters with your species, I find an incredible variety of misinformation regarding myself and my race on sale for public consumption. Just look at these articles."

Expressionless, Mildred scanned the headlines: "I Bore Cur's Child," "Several Members of Congress Revealed to be Curians," and "Studies Show Exposure to Curians Can Cause Hemorrhoids."

"Would you mind buying these for me? I'm sure there must be humans who would enjoy reading a scholarly refutation of the assertions contained herein."

"Sure," said Mildred. "I'll buy these. Just don't get too close to me until I know for sure about the hemorrhoids."

Once in their room, the trio began to relax. Bill and Mildred kicked off their shoes. Cur leaned back and asked, "So anything interesting happen to you guys lately?"

"Well," began Bill, "let me see. After playing Good Samaritan to a space alien, I'm taken from my home and subjected to two weeks of interrogation and isolation. But I guess it wasn't as bad as two weeks at the shore in the rain. Millie here has to go through several weeks of sensitivity training to help her get along better with hamsters. Other than that, our lives have been typical of most people's around here."

After several minutes of small talk, Bill became serious. "Cur, your coming has obviously changed our lives forever, and Millie and I just can't help but wonder if your being here is really an accident. Is it possible that you're on Earth to fulfill some higher purpose?"

Cur was silent for a moment and then replied quietly, "You know, throughout the universe there is a basic principle that says nothing just happens; everything has a purpose—although that purpose is sometimes difficult to discover."

"A purpose, eh? OK, whose purpose?" asked Bill.

Cur hesitated. "Well, you know Bill, there are certain things I can't…"

Bill leaned forward. "Whose purpose, Cur? Come on, spit it out. It's only the three of us in the room. Are we talking about God here?"

Cur was momentarily taken back by both the question and the sudden intensity he detected in Bill's voice. It was evident that the alien was becoming uncomfortable, but Bill was not about to let up. "That's it, isn't it? There, I said it, it wasn't that tough. I got it on the table. The ball's in your court, my extraterrestrial friend."

Bill opened a drawer beside one of the beds and pulled out a Gideon Bible. He tossed it toward the alien. "By now I'm sure you've read at least one version of this. I'd be interested to hear what you think."

Cur jumped up, pulled the Bible from the air, and held it close. He was obviously shaken. "Bill, are you out of your mind? You could have damaged it!"

Green was taken back momentarily by the alien's reaction, but could not resist pressing the point. "Whoa! Looks like I pressed a button here. What is it about that book, Cur? Huh? C'mon, talk to me."

Suddenly and unexpectedly, surprising even himself, Cur became angry. "Do you have any idea...?" He paused seeming to grope for the right words. "You know, you may be my best friend on this planet, but..." He stopped himself again. "Don't you think that ever since I came to Earth..."

Bill smiled and seemed to be pleased with himself. "Keep going, I'm listening. Maybe we're finally getting somewhere."

Cur fought to regain his composure. "Bill, this isn't a game. I don't quite understand what's been happening to me since I came here, but it's vital that I remain as obedient as possible. Besides, the fact of the matter is that your world has had the truth for a long time, but for the most part has chosen not to believe it. Whatever my purpose for being here, it's not to reveal truth. The human race must depend on some of its own members for that."

There was silence for a moment, and the alien felt the unfamiliar surge of another new emotion. This was the closest he had ever come to a confrontation when he felt like he was holding his own.

Bill, however, was still smiling. "Truth, huh? So we're talking about truth here."

Whatever self-satisfaction the alien might have been feeling vanished quickly. In fact, he appeared to be positively annoyed with himself.

Bill sighed and continued, "So, odds are there's a purpose behind your coming here. We have no idea what that purpose might be, but we do know it's not to disclose some great revelation of ultimate truth. All right then, we need to take this discussion in another direction, and you're right, this is not a game. I don't mind telling you that I'm personally getting more and more uncomfortable about this whole scenario."

Cur reacted defensively. "What are you talking about? Specifically, what scenario?"

Bill's answer was deliberate, as if he had rehearsed what he was about to say. "OK, let's take a step back and review the situation. I'll accept for the moment that there are certain things that you can't talk about, for whatever reason. Top on the list is religion."

He stood up and started to pace around the room. "Where are we? My wife and I have rented a motel room with an alien. A lot of people would like to get their hands on this alien, possibly just to satisfy their curiosity, possibly to kill him because they fear the unknown, or possibly because they want access to his technology. The alien meanwhile, has no idea how he got here, but thinks he may be here to fulfill some higher cosmic purpose, but he can't talk about why he thinks that."

Bill suddenly stopped pacing and gestured towards his wife. "And out of five and a half billion people presently alive on Earth, Millie, you and I are the only two this alien knows and trusts. Not only that, but he finds human behavior to be completely incomprehensible and it's up to us, two average people who used to enjoy a quiet life in South Jersey, to interpret it for him. And all that because Mr. Softy here couldn't resist helping a guy in trouble, even if the guy's an alien."

He turned again to face Cur. "And you know what, my alien friend, how do I even know if I'm doing the right thing? How do I know that your professed naiveté isn't just an act, part of some elaborate hoax? How do I know that we can trust you?"

Cur held his gaze. "You don't. But you know what, my human friend? I don't know about you either. Maybe it's the other way around. Maybe I can't trust you. And you know what else? I never realized there even was such a thing as mistrust until I found myself trapped on your lousy, stinking…" Cur stopped abruptly, and a long silence followed. He was shaking visibly. Bill simply stared at the floor.

Finally Cur began to laugh nervously. "I can't believe what I just said. Please forgive me. I'm really sorry. I don't know what got into me. Actually, you're right, I've disrupted your lives and put you at risk, you deserve better." Then, as if the moment were not awkward enough, Cur began to cry.

Bill mumbled, "Oh, for crying out loud. Don't start that stuff. If there's one thing I can't stand, it's a blubbering alien. Come on, Cur. Nobody likes a crier. Shape up!"

He looked up to see his wife staring at him with her arms folded. "All right," he muttered, "I'm sorry Cur, OK? I guess I'm having a hard time thinking clearly about all this myself. It must be tough on you too. I'm just having an awful time trying to figure it all out."

There was silence for a moment, and then Mildred said dryly, "If you boys are finished, do you think we could maybe get back to our cosmic purpose?"

Hearing no immediate response from either her husband or the alien, she continued, "You know, Cur, you may find humans to be a little weird, and frankly, I can't dispute that notion. But, no offense, you're starting to sound pretty human yourself."

Cur appeared shocked. "What do you mean?"

"Look, now tell me if I'm wrong, but I think I'm hearing that you're frustrated because you think that there's some reason for your being here. You want to fulfill your destiny, but not only can you not figure out what it is, you can't even talk about it."

Cur shrugged. "So what are you saying?"

Mildred, who rarely broke into laughter, began to chuckle. "Come on, Cur. By human standards, you've got an IQ that's off the charts. Does a country girl with a high-school education have to spell this out?"

Cur stared blankly, and Mildred threw up her hands. "Do something! Do something! Do something!"

She paused momentarily. "How can I put this? OK, there are some things that you would like to do but can't. That's life, at least here on Earth that's life. So what do you do? Would it make any sense to identify some problem that you can do something about? Is there something you can do to relieve human suffering here and now, some way to make this world a better place? After all, as long as you're stuck here, you might as well make your stay worthwhile."

Cur was thoughtful. "That's a pretty wide open question. Do you have any ideas? Not being from this world, I'm not experienced in dealing with suffering and death."

"Then let me throw out an idea." Millie was becoming uncharacteristically animated. "You tell me whether this is something you're allowed to do.

"By now I'm sure you know that countless people on this planet suffer from malnutrition for a variety of reasons. Geography, political repression, and even war often hamper relief efforts. However, none of those things would be an obstacle for your spacecraft and Curian technology. Cur, can you imagine the possibilities?"

Cur's emotions began to rise again. "That would be great! Is there anything else?"

"How about pollution? With your technology, I'm sure you could help us clean up the mess we've created, and in the meantime show us how to develop non-polluting energy sources. What about crime prevention? Disease control? The possibilities are almost limitless."

Cur turned to Bill. "You know, this is the most I've been able to get out of your wife since I met you guys." And then, looking sheepishly at Millie, "Sorry. Actually you're making a lot of sense."

Cur went on to explain that he most likely would not be much help with crime control or disease prevention, but it was obvious that he was intrigued.

He got up and took Millie's hands. "There are probably all kinds of practical ways I could get involved, but how do I get started? I don't know where to begin."

By this time Bill had come back to life. "Cur, you've got to try to go public again. As you might have noticed, your arrival here has the world in turmoil. People just don't know what to think and many are afraid and angry."

Cur's face took on that familiar bewildered look again. "Afraid?"

Bill put up his hand. "I know this all seems strange, but bear with me. Many of the nations of the world have accused the United States of hiding something. Some have accused us of appropriating your technology for our own military advantage. Almost all, with a few notable exceptions, are anxious to establish diplomatic relations with Curous."

Cur still had the look. "No offense, Bill, but I think you're exaggerating. What could I possibly have done to cause fear, anger, and international turmoil?"

Bill sighed, "How can I make you understand? It's not anything you've done. It's simply the fact that you're here, and the reasons for the fear and anger are almost as numerous as the people themselves. You've come to a world of creatures who instinctively fear the unknown and you've come at a time when many fear that mankind is about to bring some terrible calamity upon itself."

Cur broke in, "Well you know, Bill...on second thought, never mind. Are you guys proposing something?"

"Yes, we are," replied Mildred, "we think you should contact Washington. Speak directly to the President and Congress and tell them you'd like to address the United Nations General Assembly."

Cur put up his hands. "Hold it, hold it right there. Number one, my first encounter with your government did not go well at all and, number two, my press conference was a disaster. Aside from you two, I just can't seem to connect with anybody here."

"Look," said Bill, "we're well aware that you could go back to your ship, stay in orbit forever, and just watch history unfold; but I'm betting that you're flat-out incapable of doing that. Millie's right. You think you're here for a reason, it's driving you nuts that you can't figure it out, you'll do anything to move towards it, and..."

Cur put up his hands. "All right, already. Ever since I've landed here, people have been trying to get me to go to Washington. So I'll go to Washington."

Bill put his hand on the alien's shoulder. "And Cur, there are other people here with whom you will connect. It may take time, but the place to start is with the seat of power in the country where you landed."

By this time Cur's look of bewilderment had relaxed and he was smiling again. "Your logic is inescapable, but I'm here to tell you that there's a side of me that does not want to go through with this. Just show me what to do."

The Greens called directory assistance and were put through to the White House. Cur got on the line. "Hi, I'm the Curian who landed here by accident and I was just wondering if I could speak with someone in authority?"

The White House operator was polite but obviously tired. "Please leave a phone number and address where you can be reached. So far this week, we've had calls from thousands of Curs, not to mention aliens from every conceivable movie, TV show, and comic book."

Cur thanked him and suggested to Bill and Mildred that perhaps he should try a more direct approach.

The next morning, a large brown box landed on the White House lawn and, before the eyes of the world, Earth's first documented alien invader surrendered to the Secret Service and was taken into custody.

Chapter 5

IN THE PRESENCE OF MY ENEMIES?

THE INITIAL INTERROGATION seemed endless, and Cur again began to wonder if he had done the right thing when he landed on the White House lawn. As he recounted for the tenth time, as well as he could, the circumstances that brought him to Earth, everyone in the room suddenly stood erect as a tall man with obvious authority entered. Cur wasn't sure what to do, so he stood up as well.

The man invited Cur to sit down. "I trust you're being treated well?" he asked. "Do you need anything? Are you hungry?"

What a nice guy, Cur thought to himself.

"Well," Cur answered almost apologetically, "do you have any space-heaters around?"

With a sudden change of voice, the man barked, "Get a space-heater in here," and several men jumped.

He held out his hand, "I'm General Brown. I saw your press conference and I've been briefed on your activities here. I realize that you could leave at any time, and with the technological capabilities at your disposal there is no way we could stop you, so I appreciate your putting up with our precautions, many of which must seem pointless to you."

Cur, as politely as he could, acknowledged that was the case, and the general continued, "I must ask you to submit to a medical examination. We need to know if you have inadvertently brought with you any micro-organisms which might be dangerous to life on Earth."

Cur tried to explain why there could not possibly be any danger, but agreed to the general's request under one condition. "Don't do anything that's going to hurt. I don't like pain, at least not the kind you get on Earth."

The general shot back, "I'll be on site. If they do anything you don't like, don't retaliate, just let me know."

Cur was confused again, but kept his thoughts to himself. *Retaliate. Retaliate, now there's another word I can't seem to translate.*

As General Brown went on, Cur had no idea why, but he felt as if he had to sit up straight. "After the medical exam, I've arranged a meeting with the President and Congress. The President would then like to introduce you to the nation in a televised address, which he will prepare. Finally, you will be given an opportunity to speak to the United Nations General Assembly. Any questions?"

"Only one," Cur replied, "when can I start helping people?"

The general was momentarily taken back by the question. "I beg your pardon?"

"You know, do something for people who need help. That's the whole reason I turned myself in. There must be countless ways I can serve humanity."

The general was intrigued. "Then why don't you just do it?"

Cur smiled sheepishly. "The Curians are great believers in respecting the customs, traditions and lines of authority of any planet on which we are guests, but so far I haven't been able to figure out exactly how things work on Earth."

"And you came to see the government?" The general exploded into a laughter that caused Cur and everyone else in the room to jump. The general quickly regained his composure, but his expression had softened into something resembling a smile. "So you want to serve humanity. Well, none of that is really up to me, but I'm sure you'll have your chance, if you just play the game."

"Game? Did you say, 'play the game?'" Cur asked, clearly excited. "Why hasn't anyone explained that to me? Curians love games! Our favorite is a sort of cross between the human games of Scrabble and ice hockey. I'd love to introduce it to Earth. What kind of game do I need to learn here?"

At this point, the general's smile grew into what seemed to be an uncharacteristically broad grin. "You appear to be an intelligent fellow, you'll figure it out." Cur was escorted to the facility where he would be examined.

For the next several weeks, Cur found himself subjected to a battery of tests of every conceivable nature. As might be expected, the results of each medical exam were ambiguous, but the doctors had their job to do and, in fact, seemed to enjoy the process. There appeared to be almost childlike excitement on the part of some in meeting this alien visitor and in breaking new scientific ground. Cur personally found their genuine scientific interest to be curiously refreshing.

There were also psychological examinations, which Cur for the most part failed miserably. In spite of his apparently photographic memory and ability to solve complex mathematical problems mentally, the medical team found themselves deeply concerned by the alien's childlike innocence and rigid convictions regarding moral absolutes.

Finally, the day came when the tests were ended. Then began what, in Cur's mind at least, was the most agonizing part of the process, the mandatory questionnaire he was required to complete prior to leaving. It was explained that this was a standard procedure designed to assist the human race in responding to future alien encounters. Belonging to a race that values accuracy, especially in written communications, Cur spent considerable time pondering his answers, even though he seriously doubted that anyone else would ever land on Earth.

For the benefit of those readers who might someday interact with alien visitors, an abbreviated version of the questionnaire has been reproduced here (Please feel free to make copies in the event of visits by multiple aliens).

Name: _____
  (In lieu of actual, a reasonable human language equivalent will be acceptable).

My Mission here is (check one) Friendly ____ Hostile ____
  (If you checked "Hostile," skip to question 3).
  1. How were you greeted when you first arrived?
  2. Were you directed promptly and courteously to the proper authorities?
  3. Did anybody attempt to shoot you?
  4. What three things have you enjoyed most about your visit to Earth? In each case, explain why.
     A.
     B.
     C.

5. What three things have you enjoyed least? In each case, explain why.
   A.
   B.
   C.
6. Will you recommend Earth to your friends? Why or why not?

In the end, the scientific community concluded that Cur's presence posed no identifiable danger to humanity. At last a date could be set for him to meet with the leadership of the richest, most powerful nation on Earth. The alien was clearly excited and spent every spare moment working on his speech.

Times being what they were, however, he found himself accompanied continuously by a military escort. Several threats had been received from terrorist organizations, and so protection of the Curian visitor became top priority.

Several of his guards could not help but notice that every morning and evening the alien would assume a kneeling position beside his bed with his hands folded in front of his face. Most assumed that was simply some sort of alien ritual.

It might also be noted that the morning prior to his appearance before the President and Congress, he assumed that position for a longer period of time than usual. In fact, he remained that way until the appointed time, when he was ushered into a bulletproof limousine and escorted to the Congressional chambers where he was scheduled to appear.

As he entered the hall, the alien smiled and waved to those assembled. He shook hands with those close by, using the traditional Curian greeting, "Hi, how's it going?" Many of these people, in spite of Cur's medical analysis proving that he posed no danger to humans, ran to the restroom to wash their hands.

Cur hardly seemed to notice. He was seated next to the President of the United States and quickly flipped through his 3x5 cards to review his speech one last time. He leaned over to the President and whispered, "You know, no matter how many times I do this, I'm still nervous. If I were human, I'm sure I'd have to go to the bathroom."

At last, the Speaker of the House called the session to order, and Cur found he could hardly contain his excitement. Here he was, just an average guy from the planet Curous, about to address a significant segment of the leadership of the human race!

Unfortunately, Cur found the first few hours of this historic encounter to be, above anything else, boring. Following a few brief remarks by the President and several high ranking members of Congress, the program was turned over to roughly a dozen people from the entertainment industry. They alternately welcomed Cur to Earth, expounded on the contributions they themselves had made toward solving the world's problems, told jokes, and commented on their social lives.

Cur kept trying to get the attention of the President, anxious to ask him questions regarding what was, at least by Curian estimation, an extremely strange meeting. As usual, the alien did not understand what was happening, but by now had learned human custom dictates that side conversations must wait for commercial breaks.

Finally, the signal was given. Cur pulled on the President's arm. "Listen, I know we don't have much time, but you've got to explain this. Who are these people and why do they appear to have a much more prominent role in all this than even you?"

The President leaned over and whispered, "I'll explain this the best I can. You see, a few years ago we reached the point where we had to admit that a majority of the American people place much more reliance on the views of professional entertainers than on those of their elected officials. Not only that, but there was a continual public outcry over the use of tax money to pay elected officials, while nobody seemed to mind paying the entertainers hundreds or even thousands of times what we, as elected officials, were making. Well, you know, politics generally follows economics, so here we are."

Cur was about to ask another question, but the show was back on the air. He, of course, wasn't even expecting the entertainers and was perplexed that the public apparently gave such credence to what they had to say. To be sure, many of the cultures encountered by the Curians had people who were designated as entertainers. However, Cur could not quite grasp what those on Earth had contributed to mankind, especially in light of their tremendous wealth, which the general public appeared perfectly willing to accord.

Anticipating the question, the President leaned over and whispered, "We had to invite them to get the ratings up." A man in uniform tapped him on the shoulder. "Excuse me sir, you had your turn."

At last, Cur was called to the podium.

"Mr. President, members of Congress, honored guests. It is a special privilege for me to appear before such an extinguished...uh, sorry, must be a malfunction in my language assimilator. I meant, of course, distinguished assembly." Cur laughed nervously and could not help but notice that he was the only one in the room to do so.

"I'd like to begin with a humorous story we tell our young people on Curous, because it teaches some important lessons on life."

People all over the world were watching, except for those who did not own television sets or refused to miss the Godzilla Christmas special. Network sponsors were sweating.

"It seems this Bessalonian was in a diner having lunch. He called to the waiter and said, 'Excuse me sir, but there's a flurpazoid in my soup.' The waiter came over and said, 'Have you taken time to consider the greater good that might come of this? Very often, what initially seems to be a problem is really a door of opportunity that might otherwise not have been open to us. If you wish, I would be happy to explore the possibilities with you.'

"The Bessalonian apologized for his short-sightedness and a stimulating discussion ensued. It turns out that the flurpazoid was familiar with several quantum equations with which the Bessalonian was not; and so the Bessalonian not only was able to expand his knowledge of the cosmos, but he made a new friend."

Cur continued, "Now within this extremely funny story, is…a." He noticed that most of the audience was not laughing, but staring blankly ahead. "I don't understand, that always gets a reaction on Curous." The alien again began to laugh nervously. This time, however, one of the sound technicians, realizing that he had missed his cue, pressed a button, and the room was flooded with prerecorded laughter. Instantly, the audience began to laugh as well, realizing that was what was expected of them.

Encouraged somewhat, the alien continued. "Anyway, as I was saying, if you look closely, there's a lesson in that story. When I first arrived on your world, I would have rather been anywhere in the universe but here. No offense intended. I also learned that many of you were upset by my coming. But since then, I've come to the conclusion that my being here can work to our mutual benefit.

"I invite you, in fact I invite the governments of the world to tell me how I can best serve the human race. I am now a permanent sojourner on your world and I desire very much to contribute to the relief of human suffering. As you may know…"

A professional athlete rose to his feet and interrupted. "Wait a minute. What do you mean you would have rather been anywhere in the universe than here? Explain yourself, alien."

Cur was taken back and, somewhat to his surprise, began to feel anger. "Excuse me sir, I believe I have the floor and I am still within my allotted time."

The athlete shot back, "Who cares what some alien has to say? Besides, who's getting paid more here, you or me?"

Several in the crowd shouted their approval.

Attention shifted to the President, who stepped to the microphone. "Mr. Cur, the United States is honored by your offer. First thing tomorrow morning, I'm appointing a bipartisan committee to study your request."

It may be that the President should have stopped there but, for whatever reason, he seemed compelled to continue.

"I know how some in the room feel, but let me ask what you, as an outside observer, would recommend that we ourselves do? All people of good will would like to see the end of disease, starvation, and bigotry, and yet, while this administration has made tremendous progress, those problems persist."

Cur flipped through his 3x5 cards. "Let's see, hold on a second. OK, I wasn't going to bring this up right away, but, uh, basically, Mr. President, for starters, the people of this great nation, along with people all over the world, need to repent."

A murmur of confusion filled the room as Congressional aides scrambled for their dictionaries and laptop computers, but Cur continued, "You see there are certain things that will bring blessing on a nation, or for that matter your world, and certain things that will bring a curse. Let me give you some examples.

"I'll start with the negative. A large percentage of your population has enslaved itself to violence, lust, and unrestrained hedonism..."

As Cur spoke, an undercurrent of murmuring began to ripple through the crowd. Some took offense at the alien's comments and others asked those sitting nearby to explain what he was talking about.

An elderly actor rose to his feet. "Excuse me sir, but what I believe you're going to suggest may work other places in the universe, but not on Earth. Some of us remember a time when people embraced such simple-minded notions of right and wrong, but we've grown beyond that. In fact, I'm proud to say that the men and women of my profession are active promoters of violence, lust, and unrestrained hedonism. People enjoy those things and they're willing to pay good money to get them."

Many in the room cheered. Several rose to their feet and demanded that Cur use his alien technology to do something about real issues, such as the threat of global cooling. Few seemed to notice that Cur was beginning to lose his composure. He momentarily turned to the side, fists clenched. "Please, please let me say it just once!"

The President got up and took Cur's arm. "Are you OK? Who in the world are you talking to?"

A young talk-show host, renowned for her insight into controversial issues, rose to her feet and put up her hands. The crowd grew silent as she spoke. "I think we should, like, hear what the alien has to say." Many in the room nodded their approval.

Cur continued with his prepared remarks, but unfortunately did not get very far. As he began to speak regarding the critical importance of seeking after righteousness, he noted that it was wrong to end the lives of babies as well as the elderly who had advanced beyond their perceived usefulness to society (a common practice at the time due to what many perceived to be economic necessity). His comments were abruptly cut short by a siren, which was so loud almost nothing could be heard above it. People came running into the room from every direction, bearing cameras and recorders.

When it finally stopped, Cur turned to speak with the President, but he was gone. Instead, a member of his staff greeted Cur. "I'm sorry, but the President had to leave suddenly. I'm here to answer any questions you might have."

Cur put up his hands. "Just one. What's going on? What was that siren?"

The aide looked grim. "I hate to say this, but you're in a lot of trouble. That siren was the intolerance alarm. The alarm is pulled in the event someone is perceived to say something that implies that a certain, say, action or behavior is bad, thereby causing mental anguish to those who engage in it."

The aide began to turn away, but Cur restrained him. "Wait, please tell me what happens now."

"These kinds of crimes are tried in the press."

Cur was even more stunned. "Tried in the press? Whatever that means, surely I'll be found innocent!"

The man shrugged. "Possible in theory, but I don't think it's ever happened. Anyway, you can expect to be the center of public outrage for at least the next ninety days, possibly more. After all, you're not one of us."

Cur's voice began to rise again. "What's going on here? Doesn't anybody realize that I only want to help people and that I have so much to offer? Doesn't anybody care about reality, about the truth?"

The aide smirked, "A great man once said, 'What is truth?'"

Someone else broke in, "We're deeply concerned about truth, alien, as long as it's entertaining."

As Cur looked around, he noted that the outrage had already begun. Several in the crowd were on their feet shouting from the floor, trying hard to get the attention of the cameras.

At this point the House Speaker stepped in to restore order. He confronted the alien. "If this is one of your Curian jokes, sir, it is in poor taste."

Cur assured him that it was not.

The Speaker apologized to those assembled, "When we asked this alien to come here today, we had no idea that he would use the occasion to badger us with alien propaganda. I would not be surprised if this is some sort of pre-invasion tactic, possibly an attempt by the Curians to break down the fabric of our culture as a step towards conquest. For whatever reason, this outsider would obviously like to undo the progress we've made during the past several decades."

He concluded by addressing Cur directly. "In the future, please keep your alien ideas to yourself. We're not as gullible here as you seem to think."

The major networks promptly switched from live coverage to an analysis of Cur's remarks by prominent political observers. Most television viewers, however, at this point changed channels to catch the final segment of a recently modernized version of *A Christmas Carol*. Bill and Mildred (who secretly preferred the original version) made the switch just in time to see Scrooge reformed and Tiny Tim say, "Random chance bless us, every one."

Strangely enough, when recording Cur's appearance, the news cameras failed to pick up a significant number in Congress and even a few professional entertainers who actually applauded Cur's remarks. It can only be assumed that was an unintentional oversight. Fortunately, however, it was reported the next day on talk radio.

The Secret Service agents who had been assigned to him, meanwhile, escorted Cur out of the auditorium. He was returned to his motel room where he remained heavily guarded. He agreed to have his calls screened due to the large number that were violent and threatening.

The following day he received an unexpected visitor.

Cur instinctively stood at attention. "General, uh… General… sorry, I can't…"

"So, you remember my title but not my name? Well relax, my other-worldly friend, this is not an official visit, and the name, by the way, is Bob, Bob Brown."

Cur invited the general to have a seat. "You know, Curians may be bad on names, but we do have tremendous respect for authority."

Cur thought he detected a brief grin and heard the general mumble, "How refreshing." Brown leaned back, cupping his hands behind his head. "You know, along with the rest of the world, I saw the upheaval you caused today. No offense Cur, you may come from a race whose scientific achievements are far beyond our own, but your political skills stink."

Cur appeared to be deep in thought. "You're saying I haven't learned to play the game."

The general nodded and his face momentarily contorted into that huge smile that seemed so uncharacteristic.

Cur leaned forward. "Tell me general, what am I missing? Am I the enemy of this world because I tell the truth?"

For just a moment the general's features seemed to soften again. "There are times when I've had to ask myself a similar question. I don't have a good answer for you."

"Then, if you don't mind, let me ask another question."

"Fire away," the general grunted. "And then there's something I've got to tell you."

"You say I have poor political skills, that I need to learn to play the game. But what could possibly be so complicated about, let's say, feeding starving people? Why does that need to be studied by a committee?"

"I think you already know the answer," the general snapped. "It's one of those things you can't talk about. Well let me tell you about this thing you can't talk about, this problem that only exists on Earth. We don't need you to solve the hunger problem. The nations of the Earth could eradicate malnutrition using less ink than it takes to fill a pen, but we don't do it. And so in spite of heroic efforts by some very brave men and women, the problem persists and will continue to persist. In fact, it's not unheard of for leaders of nations to use starvation as a weapon to achieve their own ends."

Cur's face took on a look of utter disbelief, and for a long moment there was silence.

Brown stood up and began walking in a circle. "Here's what I came to tell you, and if you don't mind, I'd rather you didn't discuss this with a lot of nosy newspaper reporters, at least not yet."

He paused for Cur's response. The alien shrugged. "Whatever you say."

The general resumed walking. "A few weeks ago, we picked up a series of indistinct objects several hundred thousand miles beyond the orbit of the moon. As we observed them, they seemed to hover for days at a time and then in unison move together in clearly discernible patterns."

The general paused again, and Cur said quietly, "The Curian fleet. They're still waiting at a safe distance hoping to find me somewhere other than here."

The general resumed walking, this time more briskly. "Not any more. You see, we assumed that those objects were Curian ships, but took no action until your meeting yesterday with our government. Following that meeting, some powerful people decided that any race of beings with such narrow moral and ethical views had to be considered a threat, and so a message was broadcast into space in the direction of your fleet."

Brown stopped and simply stared for a moment. Cur was on his feet. "General, what did the message say?"

Brown put a huge hand on the alien's shoulder. "It said, and I quote, 'stay away from our planet, or we'll blast your alien hides out of the sky.' Your friends apparently got the message, because the objects disappeared shortly after the transmission would have arrived. I'm sorry Cur. I don't know what this means exactly as far as you're concerned, but I need you to know that the action was completely contrary to my personal recommendation."

Cur sat down again, stunned, not quite knowing what to say.

Brown grunted half-laughingly. "Actually, I wouldn't be surprised if they were still out there, cloaked or something. I mean, let's be serious. From what I've seen, we don't have anything that could possibly be effective against a Curian spacecraft. Our message must have appeared ludicrous to them."

Cur stared ahead blankly. "On the contrary. In the collective memory of our race, no Curian has ever received a message even remotely like that one, except possibly as a Foffozyllian practical joke, and even the Foffozyllians would have chosen different words. The commanders of the Curian fleet were undoubtedly bewildered and frightened, especially in light of the origin of the signal. Yes, General, there's no question, they're gone."

Brown began to pace again, his hands behind his back. "You're sure?"

Cur continued to stare. "I'm sure."

Still pacing, the general resumed his usual staccato manner of speech. "I want to say something else. As you know, I've been thoroughly briefed on you, Cur. As I said before, I think you know exactly what's wrong with this world, you're just shocked by the extent of it. Well let me tell you something, I have seen more of the horror of evil in this world than you can imagine, and most nights I can't sleep wondering how much I've been a part of it."

He paused momentarily. "What I'd really love to know someday is, what must it be like to live in a world without pain and death? Do you think there's a chance that mankind will ever know?"

Cur began to fidget, like a man who desperately wanted to say something, but couldn't get it out. "There is a way you can know, but…"

The general abruptly stopped pacing. "I know, but you can't tell me what it is. Thanks anyway."

As the general spun on his heels and walked towards the door, Cur said he would pray that some other human being would love him enough to answer his question. He wasn't sure if the general heard.

Chapter 6

BABY, IT'S A WILD WORLD

A FEW DAYS LATER, Cur was informed that arrangements had been made for him to appear before the United Nations General Assembly. This time, however, his remarks would not be unrestricted. He was to be given a lengthy list of do's and don'ts and several hours of priming by experts in international affairs. If the United States was no place to speak freely, the United Nations was even less so.

The President of the United States, under considerable pressure from the international community, had gone to great lengths to arrange for this historic meeting. It was critical that the alien visitor in no way offend any of the delegates. That meant no comments regarding religion, morals, or lifestyles. While it was true that representatives of a few nations expressed guarded approval of the alien's comments regarding moral principles, most of the

Western nations found them either incomprehensible or highly offensive.

Cur tried his best to be patient as his coaches explained that the United Nations was founded on pluralism. The international community could not risk someone from outside this world making statements to the effect that one way of thinking was right and another was wrong. They stressed that on Earth, there is no right or wrong. What is right for one person might be wrong for another, and vice versa. Cur answered as politely as he could that this was the stupidest thing he had ever heard, but since he was a guest on Earth he would comply with their wishes. He assured his hosts that, his present record notwithstanding, he would honestly try to not say anything that might offend anyone.

The next morning he was escorted in the usual bulletproof limousine to the UN building.

This time there were no preliminary speeches and Cur was immediately invited to make some opening remarks, after which there would be time for questions.

He stepped to the podium, appeared to organize his notes, looked around nervously, and began. "Good morning, I've been advised to dispense with my customary opening joke, and so I, uh, are there any questions?"

For those readers desirous of a detailed account, the question and answer session is presented here in its entirety. Those not so inclined may wish to skip ahead.

> DELEGATE: Can you tell us where you're from?
> CUR: Yes, I'm from another planet. It's a nice planet, which is not to say that Earth isn't nice. My planet's name is Curous.
> DELEGATE: How is it that you came to Earth?

CUR: Actually, I'm not sure.
DELEGATE: Do you have a message for our world?
CUR: Uh, no, I'd, uh, really better not, not today.
DELEGATE: What technology have you given the United States, and how much did they pay you?
CUR: None, and nothing.
DELEGATE: It is known that General Brown visited you recently. Surely this was not just a social visit.
CUR: Actually it was, the general's a friendly guy when you get to know him.
DELEGATE: What are your plans?
CUR: I don't know.
DELEGATE FROM GREAT BRITAIN: Are you the blokes who have been making circular patterns in our fields?
CUR: No.
DELEGATE FROM GREAT BRITAIN: Do you know about these patterns and, if so, what causes them?

Cur looked nervously at his prompters waiting in the wings, who signaled that it was OK to answer.

CUR: Well, A space-traveling race of people who call themselves Zurkidians have been sending unmanned probes to photograph the stunning natural beauty of your planet. Being a species that is highly sensitive to matters of etiquette and good manners, the Zurkidians feel that it would be extremely impolite for them to conduct those activities without leaving some token of their visit with the people of Earth.
DELEGATE FROM GREAT BRITAIN: Assuming I believe you, what do those symbols mean?

CUR: Well, Zurkidian communication is highly complex, technical, and not easily rendered into what verbally communicative species would consider language. However, one might loosely translate the symbols you're finding to read something like, 'We love you, have a great day.'"

ANOTHER DELEGATE: Have invisible Curians been visiting Earth for the purpose of hunting humans?

CUR: No.

DELEGATE: To your knowledge, has any alien race been doing that?

CUR: Nobody of whom I'm aware. Where do you people come up with this stuff?

DELEGATE: In light of your broad experience, which includes, you've said, encounters with many other civilizations and cultures, what would you consider to be the ideal system of government?

Cur was taken back at having received a substantive question, and, being a creature with lateral vision, could not help but see out of his left eye the expressions of panic on the faces of his advisers. Being certain, however, that he could answer the question safely, he briefly held out his left hand and signaled a "thumbs up."

He cleared his throat, smiled and replied slowly; "Since I'm under orders to not offend anyone, let me just say this. If human nature were different, any system could be workable. Without a change in human nature, no system offers lasting solutions."

The words were scarcely out of his mouth when an alarm sounded, similar to the one he had heard in his address to Congress, but different in pitch. He was later informed that this was the offensive comment alarm. Once sounded, the responsible party must from that day forward wear an offensive comment headband. That is to ensure that no matter what his or her accomplishments in life, the only thing to be remembered will be the offensive comment.

Cur was flustered. "What! What did I say? I tried to be so careful."

Security guards came running from every direction and converged on the alien. As he was being escorted out of the hall, Cur found his PR manager.

He grabbed his arm. "What did I...?"

The man was in a rage. "How could you be so stupid? You couldn't stop at offending one group, just one segment of humanity, could you? You had to offend the entire human race! How could you stand there before the nations of the world and say, with a straight face, that there's something wrong with human nature?"

The man was now shouting in the alien's face. "We've been over this a hundred times. People are basically good. When people do so-called 'bad' things, it's not their fault. It's something in their environment. Boy, you really blew it big time."

Cur finally made it back to the limo and then to his motel room. Once inside, he fell on the bed and stared at the ceiling wondering whether he would ever discover his reason for being on this insane world and whether he could ever again risk speaking to anyone.

Most commentators considered the historic meeting between the alien visitor and the United Nations to be a monumental failure, and most advertisers made it clear that they would never again sponsor such an event.

It might also be noted that later that evening, in spite of the outrage expressed in front of news cameras, Cur found himself besieged with calls from almost every nation on the globe. He was offered gifts—from women to spacious living quarters—if only he would share Curian technology in the cause of the national defense of the peace-loving nation on the phone. In most cases, he wasn't quite sure how to turn down these offers without being offensive. Finally, like many humans, he found relief in letting an answering machine screen his calls.

That was not to be the end of it, however. During the next several days Cur was visited by hundreds of people, each with his or her own agenda. Some were officials of other nations bearing gifts, again hoping to find something that the alien was willing to accept in return for his technology. Some were journalists seeking interviews, and Cur was grateful that the Secret Service screened out certain members of that profession. Many were simply individuals driven by curiosity and their own imaginations. Bill and Mildred Green, of course, had free access.

Cur was pleasantly surprised, though, by one visitor in particular. James Black identified himself as the man who took Cur and the Greens into custody that first night. He apologized for the way things were handled, explaining that he really only wanted to protect the world from some unknown contamination. In the time allotted, he took copious notes while Cur discussed industrial production on other worlds and the means by which environmental hazards are avoided.

He also introduced his brother, Justin, who had been assigned by the FBI to head a special unit dedicated to monitoring the alien's activities. Upon hearing that, Cur could not contain his laughter. "You must have the easiest job on the planet. I'm not even allowed out of my room."

Justin smiled wryly. "You could always escape through a hole in the wall."

Cur laughed politely, even though he didn't quite understand the comment.

In any case, Cur was both surprised and gratified to find in Jim Black a human being that actually possessed a teachable spirit. He later found that, in spite of the human passion for rhetoric without substance, there were people out there, both in the environmental movement and industry, who were genuinely concerned about the environment.

Although Cur enjoyed meeting people and making new friends, it wasn't long before he became frustrated with his confinement as well as the apparent lack of progress in his actually being able to accomplish anything. Not really knowing quite what to do, Cur called General Brown and reminded the general of his own observation that he had the means to leave at any time. Cur stressed, however, that as a guest on Earth, and in the United States in particular, he respected local authority and preferred to conduct himself within that framework.

Following a hurried conference with the White House, General Brown gave orders that Cur was to be released on his own recognizance, provided that he remain under close surveillance. Several members of the President's cabinet questioned the wisdom of allowing a dangerous alien to roam freely. Brown laughed out loud in response and assured them that he himself was far more dangerous roaming the streets than the alien.

Recognizing that even an alien needs money to function in modern society, Cur was provided an allowance after, of course, he successfully completed multitudinous forms. For once, though, he didn't seem to mind the paperwork, because the day had finally come when, for the first time since his arrival on Earth, the Curian sojourner was free to explore his new home planet openly and in full view of the world. (Note: In light of the non-human shape of the alien's head, as well as his apparent lack of familiarity with human standards of conduct, the news industry consented to a waiver of the head-band rule).

Cur had decided that, upon his release, he would first explore Washington, D. C. Not only was he already there physically, but Cur was also rapidly becoming a voracious student of human history, and Washington seemed a logical place to continue his study. He eagerly toured the Lincoln Memorial, the Washington Monument, the Smithsonian Institute, and every other historical and cultural point of interest he could find. One of the things he seemed to find repeatedly was that, while Earth can be a place of unspeakable evil, it is also a place where individual men and women have displayed tremendous courage in the face of it.

In fact, Cur found himself strangely envious of the human beings he encountered, both personally and through books, who demonstrated courage and conviction under the worst of circumstances. He concluded that only in a world of pain and atrocity could he ever learn the full dimensions of virtue. This was indeed a world of striking contradictions. It was also becoming increasingly apparent that only in such a world could there ever be real heroes.

The alien also found himself anxious to meet more "real people." So far, most of his encounters with humans had been prearranged or involved heads of state who came to him with their own agendas. Surely, there was so much he could learn just walking along the streets in a highly populated area like Washington D.C., and so the alien initiated his own walking tour.

As might be expected, the reactions of people who saw Cur were mixed. Initially, almost everybody backed away. After all, they had read some disturbing things about this alien intruder.

On several occasions that day someone shouted something about the "alien invader." Each time this happened, Cur would look positively annoyed.

Finally a young woman approached. Cur stopped and waited as she spoke slowly and somewhat shyly. "Excuse me, but do you mind if I take your picture?"

Cur consented of course. After she snapped a few pictures, a friend came over and took several shots of the young woman next to the alien. The young woman told Cur her name was Emily Gray.

Emily then asked if she could touch the alien.

Cur drew back. As he did so, the crowd around them, which was already a little nervous, jumped back a step, almost in unison. The woman, however, did not react.

Cur put up his hand. "Wait, I don't mind you touching me, but you have to promise not to hit me."

The woman tried to keep a straight face, but abruptly broke into laughter. She turned to her friend, "Cheryl, the alien monster is afraid I might hit him! This is too funny!"

The bystanders, in general, couldn't figure out whether or not they should laugh, so most just stared.

Emily regained her composure. "No, look, just a light touch, if that's OK. I mean, you're not made of acid or radioactive material or something that's going to hurt me, are you?"

Cur smiled, and some thought they detected a twinkle in his eye, although that might have been dependent on which eye one was facing. "How strong is your thirst for knowledge?"

Emily stared for a moment, then turned to the crowd. She cried out, "What should I do?"

Some shouted, "Touch him!" Some shouted, "Don't do it!" A few in the back shouted, "Kill him while you have the chance!"

Cur, meanwhile, held out his arm and pulled up his sleeve. Emily hesitated, then quickly tapped his arm. Convinced that it was safe, she touched it again and then pushed gently on the alien's skin.

"You feel pretty normal to me." Then, turning to find her friend, "Cheryl, you coward, get over here. This big bad alien's not going to hurt anybody."

Emily took hold of Cur's arm. "Listen, like, I know this is kind of pushy and I'm sure you've got all kinds of important alien stuff to do, but, uh, like I've got this paper to do for school and, uh, could you talk to me about the universe? You know, from your perspective."

Cur laughed out loud. "I would love to talk with you about what the Curians have learned regarding the nature of the universe. However, I should caution you that, based on what I've observed of the theoretical dogma and the sacrosanct presuppositions to which you people currently adhere, if you hand in what I say, you'll most probably receive a lousy grade."

Emily got in front of Cur, put out her arms, and stopped him. Trying to look into both eyes, which isn't easy when facing a Curian, she said, "I care more about hearing what you have to say than I do about getting good grades, and besides, I can always say that what I write is just one alien's opinion."

"In that case," Cur extended his arm, "I'll buy you a burger."

Emily took his arm. "I don't eat meat, but I won't be offended if you do."

"Actually, I won't be having anything. I just need to sit near a heat-source."

Her friend Cheryl, meanwhile, just followed behind, saying repeatedly, "Wow! Far Out!" (Note: At the time of those events, certain expressions from the sixties had regained their popularity).

Lunch was thoroughly enjoyable for the three, although they could not help but notice that several other patrons left quickly or asked to be moved to a seat further away from the alien. Some complained about the smell, even though it's well known throughout the galaxy that Curians are odorless.

Following lunch, Cur resumed his walking tour of the nation's capitol. People around him were still cautious, but clearly the ice had been broken and his presence was becoming more or less accepted. A few more people asked to have their pictures taken with him. There were still those, however, who pulled their children close and backed away.

At certain points along the way, Cur experienced what can only be described as a strange heaviness, when his inner energy was drained and his very thoughts seemed to be under attack. He could not be certain, but these episodes appeared to be most prevalent during exposure to certain music and literature, often music and literature having words that were not translatable into any language previously encountered by the Curians.

One day, towards the end of his intended stay in the city, he heard a scream. Turning towards the sound, he was appalled by what he found. On a crowded sidewalk, three men had assaulted a woman. She was on the ground begging for help, while at least a hundred people in the area either stood gawking or tried not to notice.

The alien found himself reacting instinctively. He ran towards the woman screaming. "What's the matter with you people! Somebody do something. At least call the police!"

No one made a move to help.

Not knowing what else to do, Cur tried to pull the woman away. As he did so, one of the men took hold of the alien's arm and struck him with enough force to send him spinning into the wall. As Cur tried to stagger back, another man pulled a knife and plunged it into his mid-section. The alien cried out in pain and fell to the ground, where he was beaten and kicked mercilessly by his attackers. One man kept vocalizing something which Cur found completely untranslatable, except for the words "alien scum." Getting just a glimpse of their faces, he saw something no Curian had ever seen before on any world anywhere in the known cosmos.

Suddenly, seemingly out of nowhere, Secret Service agents appeared on all sides. The men were taken into custody and the woman to a hospital. Just prior to losing consciousness, Cur had a vision of something indescribably monstrous laughing hideously. For the briefest moment, he found himself overwhelmed by a feeling of utter hopelessness.

Meanwhile, sensing the danger to its owner, the Curian shuttlecraft descended to a point several meters above Cur's head and bathed him in an energy beam, gradually restoring his physical strength. That done, the ship silently ascended into the sky and resumed orbit.

Cur thanked his rescuers profusely and insisted that he did not need medical treatment. In accordance with their orders, they backed off and resumed their watch.

Although the immediate danger had passed, the alien was somewhat surprised to find that his emotions continued to rage. He also found that the pain from the knife wound exceeded even that which he had felt when he was bitten by the dog several weeks before. He speculated that this might have something to do with his having been on Earth for a longer period of time.

Pondering that, and seeing that things had gotten back to normal on the city streets, he continued his walk taking every opportunity to share thoughts with those he encountered. Perhaps he needed to learn more before commencing his mission.

Meanwhile, there were others who observed the day's events with great interest and with ill intent.

Chapter 7

THE ALMIGHTY DOLLAR

THE DAY SOON ARRIVED when our hero decided to leave Washington and expand his research to other cities. As he was about to board the bus to Baltimore, he was stopped by a well-dressed gentleman who offered to drive him. The man introduced himself as Don Quarterman and said he had tons of food in storage that would spoil unless Cur could deliver it to the poor.

Cur was positively elated. At last here was a human who would help him fulfill his destiny on this planet.

The alien, however, was puzzled by the man's name and remarked that he had not yet encountered another like it since coming to Earth.

The man laughed in response. "Surely my alien friend, someone such as yourself, coming from a technologically and socially superior race, must realize that there are ways other than color to classify people."

Cur shrugged and offered to call down his spacecraft, which could travel much more quickly than any Earth vehicle. Quarterman declined however, saying that he needed to determine Cur's good faith before final arrangements could be made.

Cur, again, didn't quite understand, but then he had seen stranger things pass for logic on this world and so got into the man's automobile. They were not far from Washington when the car suddenly turned onto a dirt road and accelerated.

Cur asked as politely as he could if Quarterman was certain that this was the road to Baltimore.

Quarterman replied assuringly that they were taking a shortcut.

The car stopped in a wooded area and a dozen men with assault weapons appeared from behind the trees.

Cur leaned over to Quarterman and whispered, "I think we might be in some kind of trouble."

Quarterman simply smiled and drew a gun on the alien. "At least one of us is. Get out of the car."

Cur obliged, and as he looked around wondering what might happen next an elderly man stepped forward. He was wearing some sort of uniform on which was displayed prominently the insignia, "$1.00." The man grinned. "Good morning, Cur. My name is Doctor Greed, and you're going to make me even richer than I already am."

Cur could not help but notice that everyone else wore similar uniforms denoting various levels of currency ranging from one to ninety nine cents. The man who introduced himself as Dr. Greed was apparently their leader.

As he spoke, his voice was the coldest of any the alien had heard since coming to Earth. "Now listen, my alien benefactor, here's what you are going to do for me. You're going to call down that marvelous box of yours and we're all going to take a ride to my administrative headquarters before the authorities have a chance to stop us.

"Oh, and on the chance that you might raise an objection, I took the liberty of inviting someone else along for the ride. I believe you are acquainted with Bill and Millie Green? Well, abducting them would have been far too risky, even for me. However, I did manage to secure their daughter, along with her husband and two children. Meet Rob and Sara White and their two lovely offspring."

The family emerged and was held at gunpoint.

Greed's expression never changed. "I think you get the picture Cur. I'm told that it may not be possible to kill you. However, the same cannot be said of your friends. One false move out of you or your flying box and they will die horribly while you watch."

Cur was fighting to remain calm, "You know, I'm beginning to think I've been tricked."

Greed simply laughed. "Meeting you has given me renewed visions of the opportunities available in outer space."

Cur, his anger rising, but still determined not to say anything he might later regret, shot back, "Doctor Greed, you're nothing but a…a…a big fat stink head!"

Greed sneered, "I could have you arrested for hate speech for that. Now, the box."

"It's on its way."

Seconds later, the Curian vessel descended and landed softly several yards from where they were standing. A portal opened in the top and a rope ladder fell to the side.

As they climbed into the ship, Greed grumbled, "With all of your scientific achievements, I can't believe you creatures haven't invented an easier way to get in and out of this contraption."

"Actually," Cur replied, "most space-traveling species find that after a long space flight a little physical exertion is welcome. Now take the Wafletonns for example, the first thing they do upon leaving their ship is a dance similar to your Hokey Pokey."

Rob added, "Now you know what it's all about."

Greed remained expressionless, but Cur laughed out loud. "Hey, good one, Rob."

Once inside, Greed shoved a piece of paper at Cur setting forth their destination. Cur manipulated his controls, which were incomprehensible to the humans on board, and turned to Greed, "You know, I've been thinking about this. I'll bet that you don't even really have any food for the poor. Am I right?"

Greed's henchmen laughed loudly, but stopped immediately when their leader held up his hand. "You boys forget what I said about laughing on the job? We're here to fulfill mankind's highest calling, the accumulation of wealth, not to enjoy ourselves."

"So," Cur continued, "would you please tell me what this is all about?"

Like all master villains, Greed was delighted for the chance to explain his intentions to the captured hero. "I'm going to sell you to the highest bidder. Surely you realize by now that you are a commodity that is highly in demand, not only by many legitimate governments, but also by organizations who…how shall I say this…would like to see some sort of change in the existing world-order."

"You see," Dr. Greed continued, with the look of a man about to see his dreams come true, "I expect you to net for me a significant return on the time and resources I've invested to capture you."

Cur had that perplexed look again. "You humans are once again proving to be incomprehensible. You must realize Doctor, that the human life cycle is extremely brief and that you are nearing the end of this phase of your existence. Aren't you the least bit concerned regarding what will happen to you when your physical body expires?"

Greed sneered, "A well adjusted man never considers his own mortality."

Cur's perplexed look grew even more pronounced, but rather than debate the point, he said simply, "I hate to break the news, I mean you're obviously excited about my capture, but, uh, this is not exactly going to turn out the way you planned."

"What is that supposed to mean?" Greed snapped, and several weapons were raised and pointed towards the captives.

"It means," Cur replied calmly, "that I've contacted the authorities and I'm turning you in. We're on our way to see them now."

Dr. Greed was, of course, enraged. "You think this is some stupid game, don't you? Maybe when you see just how serious I am, you'll change your mind! Start with the husband."

Rob and Sara thanked Cur for not backing down. They were obviously expecting to die, and Cur found himself in awe of their courage.

Greed gave a signal and several shots were fired. Incredibly, however, Rob White was unharmed. Each shot was deflected by bursts of energy that seemed to emanate from all directions.

Greed shouted, "Fire again, point blank."

This time, not only did the weapons have no effect, but they abruptly ceased to function at all.

Greed reacted like a child throwing a temper tantrum. "This isn't fair! It's just not fair! Why would the Curians, a race of goody goodies telling stupid jokes, have developed such a sophisticated defense system if there's no war and no crime where you come from?"

The alien gazed at his human enemy, and began to chuckle. "You've been doing your homework, haven't you, Doc? Can I call you Doc? How is it that I can't seem to get the good guys to listen, but the bad guys remember everything I say? And by the way, just for future reference, I'm not from your planet and even I know never to end a sentence with a preposition."

Cur rambled on while Greed simply stared, his fists clenched. He was obviously a man accustomed to getting his own way and did not enjoy being bested by this simple-minded alien.

"Anyway, it's not a defense system in the sense that you use the term. Interstellar travel can be extremely hazardous and unpredictable, and so, in cooperation with other space-traveling races, we've developed systems to protect the occupants of our vessels from any eventuality. The ship was simply doing what it was designed to do."

"Besides," Cur went on, "as other humans have at times noted, one should never engage an enemy on his or her own turf." He paused. "Although the fact is, I don't like having enemies. Maybe someday you and I could be friends."

Greed mumbled something that Cur was not able to translate.

The alien extended his hand. "Listen, I read something recently that I think you should consider. It was written by a very wise human whose name was uh...uh, rats, I can't remember. Anyway, he said 'ill-gotten gains do not profit, but righteousness delivers from death.'"

Greed sneered, "It's bad enough that you're an alien, but do you have to be a Bible-quoting alien?"

Shortly thereafter, they landed and Greed and his staff were taken into custody. As he was being led away, Greed turned and in a voice even more icy than before shouted, "You're going to pay for this, you alien freak."

Cur turned to Rob and Sara, "You know, that guy really needs to see the big picture. Can I give you folks a lift home?"

Although the Whites did not want to impose, their children begged for another ride in the spaceship. Cur was glad to oblige, and treated them to several orbits of the Earth, finishing with an unusual aerial maneuver that had the children begging for more.

As the ship landed, Sara sighed, "You know they're not going to sleep tonight."

Cur was still a little rattled by his encounter with Dr. Greed. He asked the Whites if they could tell him more about him and his organization. He was invited in, and, after the children were in bed, Rob and Sara had coffee while Cur sat by the stove.

"Greed is an insidious man," Sara began, her voice betraying anger. "His goal, and that of his organization, is quite simply to generate income both for it and its membership. Now I'm not saying that there is anything wrong with that per se. Many of us in America remember when this was a country that rewarded achievement and contributions to the overall good. Greed has taken what used to be called the American dream and perverted it."

As Sara spoke, Cur was intrigued that her mannerisms were so much like those of her mother. It was also apparent that her opinions regarding the subject at hand were well rehearsed.

"The Greed organization seeks the accumulation of wealth through any means possible, legal or illegal. Basically that's all there is to it, and all other Greed principles flow from this single objective. The organization's motto is 'Greed is good,' although Dr. Greed teaches that it is far preferable to generate income whenever possible in nonproductive ways. As soon as you create something of value, you expose yourself to liability and enforcement actions from the government, and so the ideal methodology generates cash flow while producing absolutely nothing of value to anyone."

Cur formed a letter "T" with his hands. "Wait a second. Slow down. You're going a little too fast for me. Why don't people simply recognize what is going on and just refuse to be a part of it? I mean, nobody is actually forced to buy into this, are they?"

Sara held up her hand with one finger in the air. "Remember Cur, you've come to an imperfect, fallen world. Now, there are several unique..."

She stopped momentarily, noticing that Cur had flinched at the word "fallen." She held her hand to her head seeming to mentally shift gears.

"Look, Rob and I know all about you from my parents, and our experiences with you so far verify everything they told us."

Rob broke in, "My in-laws have this theory that the only place there's bad people and bad things happen is here on Earth because the first two humans sinned. They think the Curians and other races out there know about evil. They know that it exists, but they have no direct knowledge of it. By coming here, you've been exposed to the knowledge of good and evil, and worse, you're becoming like one of us. That's why you can never go back. You are infected."

Cur thought he detected a little sarcasm, but of course he could have been wrong.

Sara appeared mildly irritated. "Rob, you'd better not be making fun of my parents!"

Rob only shrugged.

Sara then picked up at exactly the point where she left off. "There are several unique things about Greed's organization. One is his emphasis on scientific research. He has hired some of the best talent from industries where companies have been downsizing, and he uses this to try to enhance his public image. Of course there are allegations, never proven, of close ties to organized crime. But unlike organized crime generally, the Greed organization cuts across racial and ethnic lines."

Cur said nothing at first, and then laughed lightly. "I'm sorry, it's just that you're like a cross between your mom and a Slizobeezian research analyst. Actually, I think I've been here long enough that I can see how a guy like Greed might prosper. Almost since I first landed, I've found it curious that a large percentage of humans work extremely hard to earn money, and then spend that money in ways that advance their own destruction. I don't claim to really understand, but I think I'm beginning to see how, in a perverse sort of way, Greed's message could be appealing."

Sara smiled and got up. "Rob, do me a favor and take over? I'll try to get these kids settled down."

Rob put down the cup of coffee he had been nursing. "Believe it or not, most of what Greed does is not violent in a physical sense. He apparently was willing to try something as brazen as kidnapping you because he saw tremendous profit potential."

Cur cleared his throat. "Another question—what do those currency figures on their uniforms mean?"

"Those numbers signify rank, which is, as you can see, measured in monetary terms."

Cur grimaced. "Measuring the value of a person based on a medium of exchange? What a revolting thought. I certainly hope it's not widespread. Anyway, it's certainly good to know that Greed character is in custody and out of commission."

"Don't bet on it," Rob replied tightly, "he has some of the best lawyers in the country working for him."

Cur appeared exasperated. "What possible difference should that make? He lied, an act in itself unthinkable anywhere but here, and then he actually tried to kill you! Isn't that enough to warrant removal from society? And why should people trained in law, which, by the way, is universally recognized as a good thing, want to subvert justice?"

Sara had reentered the room. "To quote my father," she replied quietly, "welcome to Earth."

Cur winced, remembering the last time that he heard someone say that.

Chapter 8

THE DOLLAR REBOUNDS

Cur soon discovered that Rob and Sara were correct. Greed was released. There were no laws that specifically addressed mistreatment of aliens, and so technically no crime had been committed. If Cur were human or animal, the outcome might have been different.

Regarding the attempted murder of the White family, there were no witnesses other than the victims themselves, and their testimony was considered doubtful due to their account of the incredible, but unverifiable, protective capabilities of the alien vessel.

However, all of that paled in comparison with Cur's discovery that several pieces of equipment were missing from his ship. Needless to say, that was incomprehensible to his human friends, especially to the White family, who owed their lives to Curian defense systems. Cur explained as well as he could, both to them and to the police, that with all of their technological advances in creating systems to protect life and property, the Curians never had a need (until now) to defend against theft. To his dismay, Cur discovered that stealing, like lying, is one of those things that may be unthinkable in the rest of the universe, but is practiced freely on Earth.

Unfortunately, there was no direct way to discover what had become of the stolen items. News of the theft was, of course, reported immediately to the FBI and the United States military, and there was concern among some that a super-weapon might be unleashed that would destroy civilization. Under intensive questioning, Cur gave every assurance that this was not possible.

There was also concern in the highest levels of government that panic might erupt if the news ever became public. Unfortunately, it wasn't long before fear became reality.

Gangs of "Curian" thugs began to appear in several major cities across the United States, committing daring daylight crimes and leaving terrified victims to tell their stories on the evening news. Every effort by police to stop them was thwarted. Bullets bounced off invisible force fields while getaway cars, which appeared to be standard models, mysteriously gained the power of flight.

News analysts had no explanation as to what need aliens might have for paper currency and negotiable securities. Repeatedly however, this is what was demanded and taken. It was also noted that while the "Curians" subjected many of the victims of their crimes to severe threats, no one was ever actually harmed.

Despite the unanswered questions, two trends were becoming increasingly evident. Tremendous wealth was being accumulated somewhere and the public's fear of Curians had begun to increase geometrically.

As a result, Cur was no longer free to come and go as he pleased. He moved back into his spacecraft, while the Greens and the White family were moved to a federal facility and guarded continually.

Cur was informed that several speaking engagements at major universities had to be canceled because of student protests. When he suggested that those institutions ought to foster the free exchange of ideas, he was told to keep his alien ideas to himself.

Not knowing where else to turn, Cur sought out the Greens. He was asked for identification, and then granted access to them just in time to catch the 6:00 news. Government spokespeople insisted, as they had from the beginning, that the criminals were really humans and that they were using devices stolen from the alien's spacecraft. Nevertheless, men and women in televised interviews on street corners and bars across the country insisted that this explanation was only a government cover-up. At least, those were the interviews that survived the cutting room.

The alien was incredulous. In the interest of good manners, he waited until a commercial break and then exploded. "Help me out here, folks. Has the human race really fallen this far? Isn't it obvious to the most casual observer that those guys are humans dressed up like Curians? Is mankind really that anxious to believe the worst about me and my species?"

Suddenly, Bill put his hand up. "Hold it a second Cur. Do you believe this?"

There, before the eyes of the world was Doctor Greed surrounded by reporters and cameras.

"Doctor, is it true you had an encounter with the alien called 'Cur'?"

"Yes I did, and please allow me to explain. Frustrated by the bureaucratic inaction of our government, I attempted to resolve this crisis myself. I was in fact successful in capturing the alien invader, but was thwarted by the very government sworn to protect us. Believe it or not, I was taken into custody, while the alien invader was released to wreak havoc on our world.

"With all that as background, you can see why I am so deeply hurt by allegations that I am somehow responsible for those space creatures terrorizing innocent human beings. After all, this is our world."

Cur was sputtering, "H...how can he say those things? How can he even get the words out?"

Bill put his hand up again. "Come on Cur, what else do you expect from a guy who kidnaps you and then tries to kill my daughter and her family? Now hold it a second, I want to hear the end of this."

Greed was still being interviewed. "Now I know that not everybody agrees with everything I do, but I'm here to say that from this point on I'm dedicating my life and whatever resources the Greed organization has to offer to ridding the world once and for all of this alien menace. It's time to restore human pride. Who will join me? Earth for the humans!"

Several bystanders, whom Greed had paid to be there, were cheering and clapping.

Cur was sputtering again, "Bill, you've got to explain this to me, and please take it slowly. Why is this guy getting air time, and why are people applauding what he says?"

"Come on, Cur. You knew that Earth was a bad place when you landed here. You told me so yourself. In fact, go back to what you told me General Brown said. You're just surprised how bad it really is. Besides, like it or not, here on planet Earth, money talks."

"Yeah, you're right," Cur responded quietly. "I guess I shouldn't be surprised by anything."

Cur was silent for a moment, and it was obvious his thoughts were somewhere else. Then, as if coming back to reality, he stood up and said, "I must stop them. Oh, and one other thing, do you guys think you could forgive me for some inappropriate comments about you and your world that I've made along the way?"

Bill blurted out, "What? Are you kidding?" Bill, Mildred, Rob, and Sara assured him, of course, that they had.

Mildred concluded, "Actually, based on what you've been through, I'd say you've had the patience of a saint."

Cur's eyes widened (or at least the eye that Mildred could see). "Patience of a saint, huh? Hmmm, interesting expression. Anyway, whatever, I still need to stop those phony Curians from victimizing people. So if you'll excuse me, I'm going back to my ship to continue my search."

"Let me save you some time," Rob interjected, "it just came over the news that they've been spotted in Atlanta, Georgia."

Bill took hold of Cur's arm. "Hold it, I'm going with you."

The alien pulled away. "Sorry, my good friend. Too dangerous."

Bill began to mutter something and then noticed that his wife was fighting to hold back tears.

"Oh for crying out loud, Millie, cut it out! You're supposed to be the strong one in this family."

"I can't help it Bill, I just have a very bad feeling about this."

Cur, meanwhile, quickly climbed the rope ladder into his ship, which was hovering outside, and in an instant he was gone.

He arrived in Atlanta seconds later to a scene that was becoming distressingly familiar. Several apparent Curians armed with automatic weapons and laser rifles had just finished robbing each of the large center-city banks and were preparing to make their escape. As usual, the police were powerless to stop them, being unable to penetrate the invisible force fields that surrounded the "aliens."

Not finding a place to land in all the commotion, Cur parked his spacecraft about twenty feet above the ground and descended his rope ladder.

He walked over to the officer in charge. "Excuse me, but could you use a hand?"

The man was incredulous. "Look buddy, do you have any idea what's going on here? Now why don't you take off that Cur outfit before somebody here shoots you."

Cur laughed and held out his arms. "Hey, look at me! Does this look like a costume? I'm the real Curian, the only Curian on this, this fine planet of yours. Those guys are only dressed up to look like me and they're using devices stolen from my vessel. I think I can stop them if you let me. Now, do you happen to have a tire iron I could borrow?"

The officer stared at Cur for a moment, then mumbled, "I should have listened to my father and sold real estate. Sure pal, I'll get you a tire iron. Just promise me you won't hit anybody with it."

Cur's face twisted into its now standard look of perplexity. "You mean people on Earth use these things to hit each other?"

The officer answered matter-of-factly, "You'd be amazed at what people hit each other with down here, alien," and handed Cur what he requested. "You're gonna break through the force field with a tire iron?"

"Actually, it will let me in. It knows me. Now, one more favor, ask your men to stop shooting while I try to save the city?"

As Cur ran towards the scene of the crime, he thought he heard the officer mumble something untranslatable, which he recognized from previous encounters with humans in stressful situations. His curiosity regarding that would have to wait, however, while he attended to the more pressing matters at hand.

Meanwhile, the "Curian" criminals began moving toward their getaway car, carrying the money they had stolen. One of them, a woman, held the force field device.

She saw the alien coming and turned it in his direction. As Cur had predicted, however, the force field opened and let him pass. And then while the police and bystanders, not to mention the criminals themselves, watched in utter bewilderment, Cur ran towards the vehicle and loosened the lug nuts on one of the tires.

A shrill female voice rang out, "Kill it!"

For a brief second, the force field disappeared, and a volley of bullets and laser bolts pounded Cur's body. He screamed in pain as the force of the attack threw him back. Before the police could react, the force field was turned back on, and the gang dove into the automobile. The engine roared to life but the car moved only several yards and stopped.

A female voice was again heard above the din. "What's the matter with this thing? Why won't it fly? We saw that alien doing something to the car, he must have planted some device, get out and look for it. You'll be safe as long as I maintain the force field."

The entire area was becoming chaotic as law enforcement officials and television crews converged on the scene. Cur, meanwhile, was bathed in a tightly focused beam of energy that emanated from his ship, still hovering overhead. Surrounded by police officers and rescue crews, he summoned the strength to speak. "Please listen," he gasped weakly, "my ship is programmed to attend to me. It will bathe me in energy that will facilitate my healing. But it will ignore the attackers. You must stop them."

"Stop them, but how?" blurted several voices. "Everybody knows that nothing can penetrate a force field."

"Think," Cur whispered, "can you see them?"

The commanding officer jumped and hit his fist. "He's right! It's so obvious! Heat and light can pass through that field. If radiant energy couldn't get through, we wouldn't see them. It would be pitch black and cold inside!"

He leaned over to speak with the fallen alien. "Listen Cur, one question. I think I'm beginning to understand how that thing works. If we try to make things too hot for those people, won't it try to protect them and strike back?"

Cur smiled weakly and struggled to answer. "Normally you'd be correct. However, shortly after arriving on Earth, I programmed it to protect only Curian life. Otherwise, it would have burned out trying to respond to millions of humans in pain."

He paused to gather strength. "And Curians live by absorbing energy."

Apparently satisfied, the officer in command jumped up again and shouted, "All right people, let's see if we can make them sweat."

Within minutes several helicopters appeared armed with high-intensity searchlights. The "Curians" began to howl, blinded by the lights and rapidly becoming uncomfortably warm.

Finally, the force field went off and the police moved in. By this time, Cur had regained some of his strength and was standing. A path opened up as he staggered towards his assailants. He ripped a mask from the woman who had ordered his death and said simply, "My protective energy device, please?"

She drew close and said sweetly, "You know Cur, these people may be your friends today, but you and I both know that won't necessarily last long. Maybe someday we could be on the same side. You know, you and I could be great together."

Cur, at first, didn't quite understand what she meant, but had been on Earth long enough to figure it out. With anger in his voice, he shot back, "I have a wife, and marriage for Curians is a sacred, eternal union." Then, with the beginnings of a smile, "Besides, no offense, but I don't find you at all attractive. I prefer women with much ... larger ... noses, on the other sides of their heads."

He turned and faced about a dozen cameras that had quickly converged on him. "Hey, did you guys catch that last line? I mean, I've encountered, what's the word, *chutzpah*, on this planet before, but this woman has to take the prize!"

Immediately, reporters began to fire questions.

Cur, however, was still extremely weak. He soon became uncontrollably dizzy and fell to the ground, while the energy beam from above continued to envelop him. As rescue crews moved in, a commanding voice cut through the pandemonium. "Don't touch him! He's not like us, and the best thing we can do right now is leave him alone."

The paramedics backed away, and a tall uniformed man emerged from the crowd of onlookers. "My name is Colonel Blue and I have orders from General Brown to protect this alien at all costs."

Instantly, news cameras surrounded the colonel. "Colonel Blue, why is the government so interested in protecting this creature?"

The colonel responded as a man accustomed to public questioning. "Cur is a guest on our world and one who may offer infinite possibilities for the growth and advancement of the human race."

Another reporter shoved a microphone in his face. "That's the official line, but isn't the real reason for all this concern that our government fears a Curian invasion if anything happens to this one?"

"No, that is not an issue," he answered coolly. "Number one, we have evidence that the Curian fleet has abandoned the search for its missing crewman and left this region of space. Number two, Cur has maintained that he believes in returning good for evil and that all Curians share his perspective."

Laughing sarcastically, the same reporter asked, "Come on, Colonel, do you take us for fools? Nobody thinks that way."

Another reporter pushed her way to the front. "Colonel, there have been reports of Curians entering human bodies and taking over their wills. What, if anything, is the government doing about this?"

Colonel Blue sighed, "Madam, as far as we can determine, there is no validity to any such assertion."

Someone noticed that Cur was regaining consciousness, and he again became the center of attention.

"Have the criminals been captured?" he asked weakly.

The colonel answered, "Yes sir, they have, thanks to you."

Cur regained his footing. "Tell General Brown I said hi and that I'm still praying for him."

Colonel Blue smiled. "I'm sure the general will appreciate that."

A reporter pushed a microphone into the alien's face. "Cur, now that you've survived a brutally savage attack, can you tell our readers, how did it feel to have your body riddled with bullets while trying to change a tire?"

In a rare moment of obvious irritation, Cur was about to say something inappropriate. He caught himself, however, and instead responded, "I often find that painful experiences can also be opportunities for personal growth."

The reporter turned to the camera, laughed nervously, and said, "I wonder what he meant by that? We now take you live to a taproom in Swampville, Ohio to see what people there think about all this."

Off camera, he turned to a colleague and whispered, "Why can't this guy just whine about his problems like everybody else?"

Another reporter asked the beleaguered alien, "Police sources say that just before you were shot, you loosened one of the wheels on the getaway vehicle. What exactly were you doing at the time of the incident?"

Cur grinned weakly. "Your police sources are correct. I loosened the lug nuts on one of the wheels to make the automobile unsafe to drive. You see, all Curian devices are equipped with an automatic shutoff feature that engages any time an unsafe condition exists. The loose wheel represented enough of a danger to prevent the levitation module from functioning.

"Now if you'll excuse me, I need some R and R." Cur gestured towards his ship, and at Colonel Blue's command a space was cleared for it to land. The alien found that he did not yet have the strength to climb aboard, but he also found that humans can be compassionate as well as cruel. Several police officers and news people helped him in, and within seconds the alien vessel disappeared into the sky.

Chapter 9

THE GOOD, THE GREEDY, AND THE PERVERSE

MONTHS PASSED, AND EXCEPT FOR a few spectacular headlines in select newspapers, there were no sightings reported of the alien known as Cur. Many observers began to conclude that Cur himself was really nothing more than some sort of elaborate hoax.

In one special sense however, the alien visitor had not been forgotten. Curian jokes had replaced ethnic jokes in many circles and, no matter how tasteless, could be told with impunity. They were especially popular on late night talk shows, especially in light of Cur's public statements regarding ethics and morals.

It might also be noted that Cur's stand on those issues won him some extremely vocal opposition, with the leadership of several popular movements maintaining that Cur was nothing more than an extraterrestrial puppet of the radical Christian right.

Three enemies in particular devoted themselves to his destruction, one having already actively engaged the alien. That was, of course, Doctor Greed. Although none of his loyal followers would ever dare say it out loud, many felt that he was motivated by something other than money. Still seething from his setbacks, he called a special organization-wide staff meeting as soon as his schedule permitted.

"You know why we're here," he began, "phase one would have been an unqualified success, were it not for the alien himself. Who in their wildest imagination would have guessed that anyone these days would sacrifice himself for the sake of others? But then again, there is no way we could have anticipated his alien logic.

"Nevertheless, all is not lost. Human nature being what it is, the general public can be made to forget that they were the victims of a scam and that they were threatened not by Cur himself, but by humans disguised as Curians. We need to play upon their natural fear of the unknown and unfamiliar. If human beings can so easily be taught to hate other human beings because of superficial, racial differences, imagine the intense revulsion that can be generated toward a non-human alien!

"Now, being a loyal member of this organization, I'm sure you're thinking, *what's in it for me?* At least, that's what I hope you're thinking. So, let me remind you of one of the basic tenets of our faith: That one sure road to acquiring unearned wealth is to capitalize strategically on the dark side of human nature.

"Given that fundamental truth, the first part of my plan involves a massive hate campaign designed to generate cash flow. To that end, I've managed to forge an alliance with another force in world culture almost as powerful as our own, which will work closely with our public opinion staff. Ladies and gentlemen, welcome Dr. Pig."

Those in attendance applauded respectfully as the ugliest but most impeccably dressed man they had ever seen joined Dr. Greed at the dais.

As he began to speak, even the most hardened members of his audience found him compelling, almost to the point of being hypnotic.

"My good friends, this is indeed an historic occasion, when the forces of Greed and Pig—two of the most critical components of modern values—join forces to rid ourselves of a menace that is not even from this world. Your imperious leader and I had hoped that Dr. Ego would join us, but he, unfortunately, felt that any such alliance would compromise his, pardon the expression, principles.

"Let me assure you that the Pigs of this world view the alien as a very real threat to us and our philosophy of life, a philosophy of life that dates back to the earliest days of recorded history, and which, I might add, has brought happiness and fulfillment to untold millions throughout the ages."

Greed abruptly took the microphone. "Excuse me Doctor, but we agreed that there would be no proselytizing. Besides, Greed members are not interested in happiness and fulfillment. Our only goal is the accumulation of wealth."

"My apologies, Doctor," Pig wheezed repulsively. "I only wanted to make the point that the Pigs of this world are as anxious as the membership of Greed to eliminate the alien Cur. Believe it or not, he's actually stated on more than one occasion that people are accountable for their actions and should, in humility, put others ahead of themselves!"

Many in the audience gasped.

Dr. Greed flashed his most sincere fake smile. "I hear you, Doctor. We also have the alien on tape stating that material possessions are not the most important thing in life!"

Again, many gasped in shocked disbelief, and a few fainted.

Greed went on, "Now that we've established the seriousness of the threat, allow me to explain a few things to my associates.

"The profits from this venture will not be distributed in the usual fashion. Naturally, we'll pay Dr. Pig a fee for his services. After all, one often needs to spend money in order to make money. The rest will be reinvested in research and development. I want to find a way to destroy the alien before the eyes of the world. When that happens, we will be heroes and able to name our price. Any questions?"

A woman in the back of the room nervously put her hand up. Greed recognized her and said reassuringly, "Please relax, everything here is strictly business."

"Well sir, if we actually kill that thing, isn't there a possibility that his friends will come and attack the Earth?"

Greed appeared disgusted with the question. "I will not tolerate that kind of thinking around here. You may possibly be right, but look at it this way. If we don't defame and destroy Cur, then assuredly a competitor will and reap the rewards that would have been ours. If other Curians are so inclined, the Earth will be attacked anyway, and we'll be no better off for having held back. Any other questions?"

A large, rough looking man marked "95 cents" had his hand in the air. "How exactly we gonna make folks hate da space creature?"

Greed forced a tight grin. "An excellent question. Lenin once said that the surest way to change a culture is through its music. Dr. Pig, in cooperation with our people, is going to write a song and then follow it up with a music video."

The same man had his hand up again. "But what if da people don't like da song?"

The doctor's grin became more pronounced. "That's the least risky part of the plan. We have enough money and influence to make sure the song gets airtime. Once it has airtime, no matter how badly it stinks, millions of people will automatically believe it's good and purchase the CDs, tapes, and videos. This isn't new, it's been done successfully countless times before, in fact…"

Dr. Pig interrupted, "If I may, Doctor."

"Of course," Greed replied, attempting to appear respectful.

Pig stepped forward.

"In fact, we need to be careful to avoid the 'Q' word. The existence of quality in any endeavor of this sort not only turns off a large segment of the public but also implies that there might be other things of less quality. We certainly don't want to turn the clock back to that kind of thinking."

A scholarly looking man marked "29 cents" was recognized. "Excuse me, Doctor, but there's one part of the plan that may not be feasible. Curian technology has advanced significantly beyond our own, particularly in the area of defensive capabilities. We've witnessed the alien vessel utilize physical principles of which we have no knowledge, let alone mastery. I would submit that it may not be possible to carry out your wishes, no matter how much money we spend."

Greed took the microphone, his face red with rage. "I can't believe what I'm hearing. Go back and read your guidebook and you'll find that money is the answer to everything. You seem to have forgotten that any problem can be solved by throwing enough money at it. Your status with the organization will be reviewed in six months. In the meantime, consider yourself reduced five cents in value."

As the man left the room in disgrace, Greed pounded the podium. "This project is to have priority over all others! I don't care how it's done, but I want that alien destroyed."

Dr. Pig rose to his feet and applauded. "Here, here Doctor. Well said!" The audience joined him.

Cur, meanwhile, remained in orbit high enough above the Earth to avoid detection and was unaware of the terrible plots being conceived for his destruction. His wounds were healing, albeit at a slower pace than he had expected. Most of his time was spent observing Earth and pondering his next move. He did remain in touch with his close friends on Earth, and they, of course, were supportive.

He discovered that surfing the Internet (which at the time of these events had expanded greatly beyond its present capabilities) made the days go by more quickly. Although still crude by Curian standards, Cur found it to be fun, almost to the point of becoming addictive. He especially enjoyed researching the reference materials.

In addition, General Brown and his staff provided Cur with a steady stream of reading material covering every aspect of human life and culture. Normally, this was accomplished by delivering books and other materials to some remote location where Cur would pick them up.

It was in one of those clandestine deliveries that Cur discovered an art form that was uniquely human, the comic book. He was fascinated to read of fictional characters that not only possessed special powers and abilities, but also used them to help people in distress and fight evil in the world.

In Cur's mind however, the most exciting thing about these heroes was that they almost always functioned outside the system. They operated independently and appeared to be accountable to no one. Best of all, when the criminals had been apprehended or the world saved, there were no lengthy reports to file and no government agencies calling to tell them that they completed their forms incorrectly and had to re-file or be fined. The heroes simply showed up to do more good deeds in the next issue.

Cur had always been taught to conduct his affairs within the framework of the existing authority structure on whatever planet he found himself, but was it possible that principle didn't apply to Earth? After all, he had tried that approach, and the results to date seemed disastrous. The thought of being a superhero was just too tantalizing.

He called Bill and Millie to get their opinion, and to his surprise found them to be less than enthusiastic. Bill commented that this was the kind of idea that he might expect from his grandson, not from an adult member of an advanced civilization.

Cur was discouraged, but not deterred. Superheroes got to do good, help people, and solve problems, and some of them were aliens! True, the characters in the stories were all fictional, but until now most humans had never seen a real alien. The fit just seemed to be too perfect. Cur took it as a sign.

He designed a costume for himself, complete with cape, and flew (in his ship) to see Bill and Mildred. When he arrived, Sara and Rob were there as well. They were all obviously elated to see their friend, but had not changed their minds regarding his latest scheme to reach out and help people.

Bill tried his best to be diplomatic. "Listen Cur, did it ever occur to you that comic book heroes wear costumes to protect their identities? Who out there do you think won't figure out that you're you because of the disguise?"

Cur laughed. "Bill, Bill, Bill. That's not the only reason heroes wear costumes. Some don't even have secret identities. Now, help me with a name. I don't want to be just 'Cur' anymore. I want to be something else that will inspire a little more respect."

Rob's expression was a sort of half-smile. "Actually Cur, I think you look pretty good. How about 'Captain Curageous'?"

Sara snapped at her husband. "You're being a fat lot of help."

Although her tone was angry, it appeared to Cur that she was trying not to laugh. He could have been wrong.

"Would you even remember another name?" Mildred asked dryly.

Cur was thoughtful. He knew Millie was right. It seemed to his human friends that perhaps reason was about to prevail.

Then, abruptly, a look of excitement returned to the alien's face. "That's it!" He cried. "I'll keep the same name, but I'll be more that just 'Cur.' From now on, I'll be 'The Mighty Cur.'"

Cur ran around the room, swinging his cape and punching imaginary bad guys. Bill and Mildred continued to suggest as politely as they could that this whole idea was absurd. Attempting to appeal to his alien value system, they even warned of the dangers of false pride and an unbalanced self-image, all to no avail.

Cur had made up his mind. The world would see him again, but this time things were going to be different. Having failed to dissuade him, Bill, Mildred, Rob, and Sara simply urged him to be cautious.

The world being what it is, The Mighty Cur did not have long to wait before he made his first public appearance. Hopeh Province in China had been struck with a severe earthquake, almost of the magnitude of those that destroyed the city of Tangshan in 1976. As terrified thousands fled for their lives, they suddenly heard a voice from the sky (in their own language, of course), "Fellow inhabitants of Earth, you can relax now. The Mighty Cur will take care of everything."

Those brave enough to look back saw the alien space craft strike the ground with tremendous force and drill its way into the Earth. Minutes later the tremors ceased. The box from the sky emerged and Cur stepped out to receive the thanks of a grateful public.

He was greeted initially with stunned silence. Then suddenly the crowd began to cheer. Several shouted, "Praise the Lord," and the alien was momentarily taken back, this being the first time he heard that once familiar expression since coming to Earth.

Later that evening, the newly elected President of the United Provinces of China offered his heartfelt thanks, along with a space heater and trombone manufactured by Chinese companies as tokens of appreciation.

Not long afterward, Cur successfully rescued hundreds of flood victims in Africa, who initially were beyond the reach of human agencies. In South America, utilizing his now familiar protective devices, he assisted the police in arresting the leaders of a drug cartel. In Eastern Europe, he intervened in a civil war. In the northwestern United States, he extinguished a forest fire.

Everywhere he went, people cheered and thanked him, but he was often astonished to find anger and bitterness as well. There were almost always some that cursed him and demanded that he go home (even though he tried to explain that was impossible). *Why, he pondered, would people whom he helped respond with such hostility?* He concluded that those instances simply had to be added to his growing mental file of inexplicable human behaviors.

One day, after intervening to prevent an airline crash, Cur met an old friend among the disembarking passengers. He spotted the name "Emily Gray" on her luggage.

"Emily, hi! It's Cur. You remember, the alien guy you had lunch with in Washington."

Emily smiled coyly. "That's an old line. You can't do better than that?"

Seeing Cur was taken back, she laughed. "I'm kidding! How are you? And, oh yeah, thanks for saving my life."

Cur began to laugh as well. "I'm fine, and you're welcome. So anyway, how did you do on your term paper?"

Emily thought for a moment. "Oh, right, the paper. Well, I got an 'A.' My prof. wrote on the back that he thought you had some pretty bizarre ideas about the origin of the universe, but he was impressed that my research included a personal interview with a certifiable alien."

Cur held out his arm. "It's about that time. Want to do lunch again?"

Emily pulled back. "Under one condition. This time it's my treat. You sit by the ovens and soak up as much heat as you want."

Cur laughed. "It's a date."

During lunch, Cur explained the costume and confided that, for the most part, he was thoroughly enjoying his new role. He was convinced that the fears expressed by the Greens and Whites were proving to be greatly exaggerated.

Emily appeared to be open-minded about Cur's new identity, but kept using an expression he could not quite understand: "Hey, whatever turns you on."

A few weeks later, The Mighty Cur's first official job came. James Black (the environmental guy) managed to cut through the red tape and arrange for Cur to dispose of radioactive waste in outer space, assuming he was willing to do this. Cur, of course, was glad to oblige. He explained that, although he was not permitted to stray from Earth any farther than the distance to the moon, that was far enough to enable him to eject the unwanted material into the void of interstellar space.

Shortly after that Cur received an official request to transport food and medical supplies to several trouble spots around the world. Cur was so excited he could hardly contain himself. This was what he was hoping and praying for ever since he landed his spacecraft on the White House lawn over a year ago. From Washington's perspective, it was a win-win situation. It was good for foreign relations, and no American lives were to be put at risk.

In the meantime, The Mighty Cur found himself rapidly becoming one of the most controversial people on Earth. On the one hand, it seemed as though the tide of public opinion was finally beginning to turn in his favor. On the other, there were certain people he would never win over. That was particularly true of those who resented (what they perceived to be) Cur's efforts to impose upon the people of Earth his narrow alien views on marriage, the family, and the sanctity of life.

In balance however, most public opinion polls indicated that the alien's overall approval rating was increasing. Even the mainstream information and entertainment industry was beginning to test the waters in presenting the Curian in a less unfavorable light.

But the alien's rising public image was doomed to be short-lived because radios across the country had begun to play "The Cur Song."

Chapter 10

THE CUR SONG

IT WAS OPENING NIGHT of a weeklong engagement at the Philadelphia Spectrum (formerly the Financial Services Monolith Spectrum), and the crowd was wild with anticipation. Suddenly, surrounded by fireworks and lasers, two dozen people came running onto the stage. They varied in age from pre-adolescent to elderly. Their clothing represented several ethnic and cultural groups. Obviously, this was a performance that was intended to have something for everybody.

As the music began, the group clapped and swayed. The rhythm was penetrating in its precision and almost hypnotic. Then, one soloist after another took the microphone.

"There's an alien who's come our way.
And we think he has too much to say.
He talks about the human race.
Well it's time we showed him who runs this place!"

And then the chorus:

> "Cur has got to be destroyed.
> Cur has got to be eliminated.
> He's an enemy of this world.
> The alien must be exterminated."

The song was a masterpiece in its appeal to a wide spectrum of humanity. It combined stylistic elements of rap, heavy metal, jazz; in fact every musical genre popularized since the latter half of the twentieth-century. There was even an easy-listening version. At the same time, the chorus was repetitive to the point of being mind-numbing, which of course represented one of the primary objectives of its composers.

For the most part, Greed and Pig were careful not to use words that studies indicated would tend to produce a negative reaction in some people. Notwithstanding this, another version of the song soon gained popularity among certain segments of society and was utilized as the theme music in "Cur, the Movie."

The lyrics in this particular version may not be appropriate for all audiences and so will not be reproduced here. Suffice it to say that, in general, people in their thirties and forties favored the more violent and (by twentieth-century standards) pornographic lyrics. Their children, however, usually preferred the original version of the song and many were vocal in questioning the kind of world they were about to inherit from a generation that found it necessary to express itself using offensive language.

In any case, Greed did not want to be associated directly with the production of "The Cur Song," and so it was performed and recorded by a group who called themselves Peaceful Planet. The group was designed to be unique in a number of ways. In addition to being comprised of artists from a variety of age groups and nationalities, Peaceful Planet was the first group of recording artists in history to utilize an android drummer.

During the remainder of the Spectrum concert, the group continued its musical commentary with selections such as, "You Ain't Nothin' but a Curian," "Mamma Don't Allow No Extraterrestrials Around Here," and "Get The Alien" (to the music of 'Sink the Bismarck'). Pig's and Greed's PO staffs had performed their duties well. At the conclusion of this concert, and each one that followed, Peaceful Planet received a standing ovation.

The next several weeks only confirmed that the Greed and Pig organizations had done their homework. Peaceful Planet mania was spreading. All across the United States, and in the rest of the world as well, people were not only listening to "The Cur Song," they were singing it and dancing to it. And, just as planned, millions were purchasing Peaceful Planet CDs and music videos.

The whole world, it seemed, was talking about it, and opinions were wide-ranging. The following are typical comments, representative of large segments of the population:

> MIDDLE-AGED ADULT: Hey, I don't really listen to the words, I just like the music.
> YOUNGER ADULT: It's heavy man, I don't know what all those gorgeous babes on the video have to do with this alien thing, but I'm sure I'll figure it out if I watch it enough. I've got nothing better to do with my life.

> TEENAGER: I find the music both edifying and aesthetically appealing. If I had any criticism, it would be only that the android sings in a monotone.
>
> ANONYMOUS: If I had it my way, we'd blow up the Curian neighborhoods and start over.

Every aspect of Greed's plan appeared to be a complete success. Not only were people all over the globe beginning to hate Cur without really understanding why, but Peaceful Planet was funneling huge profits back into the Greed organization.

Even academia did not escape Greed's and Pig's relentless campaign of anti-Cur propaganda. Some of the major universities were beginning to offer courses in countering alien indoctrination.

The intellectual footings of the anti-Cur (the "pro-human" movement to its adherents) were provided by Doctor Yellow, a respected Ph.D. in alien affairs. In the preface to his best-selling book, *Why Bad Aliens Come To Good Planets* he noted:

> We should not for a moment feel guilty about ridding ourselves of the danger presented by this alien menace. Cur is not a human being and should no more be considered a human being than, say, an unborn fetus. It should be quite obvious to any thinking person that the Curians, despite their ability to travel the stars, are an inferior form of life, if indeed they can be considered life at all. Otherwise, why would Cur speak of the human race as having been created when every school child knows we evolved from slime?

To be fair, Cur had his supporters, and opinion polls indicated that they represented a significant percentage of the population. Most, however, preferred to remain anonymous rather than face the social stigma that came with being an alien-lover.

It should be noted too that there were many in academic circles that were opposed to the accepted pro-human viewpoint and saw Cur's presence as an opportunity to expand the horizons of humankind and to understand the universe in new and exciting ways. Those, however, were so severely ostracized by their colleagues that most of them chose to remain silent rather than jeopardize their positions.

Humanly correct thinking influenced even the churches. Several major denominations chose the Sunday after Easter (which, for some reason, many pastors found a depressing day) to be "Human Awareness Sunday," and services were designed to increase worshippers' sensitivity to human issues.

Again, not all churches participated, but those who did not were dismissed as being the same radical fundamentalists who still talked about sin and salvation. It was a mystery to many why those churches could not simply change their beliefs to conform to popular opinion like everyone else.

As Greed's campaign for the hearts of the world's people gathered momentum, his technical staff searched feverishly for a means to put an end to the alien once and for all. After reviewing thousands of news clippings and tapes, and gathering information from every available source, it became apparent that some field-testing was required. Not enough was known about Curian technology to determine how effective any particular form of attack might be.

Meanwhile, in spite of all the controversy, Cur was still quite visible. He continued to work with the World Health

Organization in distributing food and medical supplies wherever needed. Unfortunately, WHO found itself the target of blistering criticism from all over the world for its use of the alien's services.

Cur also continued to work with the governments of several nations, assisting them with disposal of their nuclear waste. Those nations also found themselves the target of criticism from the international community for disposing of dangerous substances in an unauthorized manner and for allowing an alien to help in the process.

Cur himself had never been happier since coming to Earth because he was doing what he really loved to do. He was helping people. And, if the truth be known, he took pride in the fact that The Mighty Cur trading cards were selling briskly in convenience stores. His compulsive altruism, however, made him an easy target.

In the weeks that followed, he was subjected to a series of attacks, which on the surface appeared to be unrelated. The first came during a mission of mercy to the Middle East, where his ship was the target of a scud missile. With the stolen Curian equipment back in place, however, the missile exploded harmlessly against an invisible force-field.

A second came in Germany, where an explosive device was hidden among containers of nuclear waste that Cur had agreed to dispose of in space. However, the ship's protective sensors detected the danger immediately, and the plot was foiled.

In one especially tragic attack, a movie theater was firebombed while Cur was attempting to enjoy the show inside. The damage might have been worse but for the fact the attackers forgot that Curians absorb energy. Most people inside the theater screamed in terror as the flames erupted and then felt a sudden chill as they were extinguished.

However, as police officers began to escort people out of the building, Cur happened upon the body of a man killed in the blast. The energy which the alien had just absorbed exploded from his body as a blinding light. He later surmised that this was the Curian equivalent of what, for a human, would constitute vomiting.

As the attacks increased in number and intensity, Greed's agents proved themselves to be professionals, and authorities appeared unable to establish a direct link between those instances and the Greed organization. For his part, Cur concluded that, for the safety of all concerned, he needed to remain in his ship.

That proved counterproductive to Greed and Pig, for it was becoming increasingly apparent that human efforts could never overcome Curian technology. If Cur was to be killed, it had to happen while he was separated from the protective cover of his ship. Needless to say, that would not be easy to arrange. After being gunned down in Atlanta and surviving the attack in the movie theater, Cur had become extremely cautious and rarely strayed far from his spacecraft.

However, Earth can be a dangerous place no matter what precautions one might take, and Cur soon encountered another human who proved to be just as deadly an adversary as Doctors Greed and Pig.

Chapter 11

I Love Me Just the Way I Am

ONE EVENING, FOLLOWING a long day of making the world safer for humanity and needing to unwind after deflecting a series of unprovoked attacks, the alien sat down next to his space heater and began channel surfing.

The phone rang and Cur was greeted by a familiar voice.

"Hey, what's happening, my alien amigo?" The voice was Bill Green's.

"Bill, good to hear from you."

"Listen, Millie and I would like to get together. How about meeting us some place you haven't been. Pick a city."

Cur was still grinning, obviously ecstatic at hearing from his friend. "Sounds good, just answer me one question. How many Mobothrakians does it take to change a light bulb?"

The voice on the other end stammered. "Uh, Three?"

The alien's expression changed to one of irritation. "Nice try, pal." He slammed down the phone.

He then tried to trace the call, but to no avail.

Mumbling something under his breath that he never would have said prior to coming to Earth, Cur went back to channel surfing.

Meanwhile, back on Earth, a well built, impeccably dressed man rose to his feet and began to pace. He stopped, pounded his fist on a rather large desk, and glared at the other men in the room, each of which could have passed as his identical twin. They stared blankly back at him.

"So," he shouted, "it appears that duplicating Green's voice was not enough to lure the alien out of that cursed ship. Now I've got to also figure out the answer to an absurd alien riddle."

He spun on his heals. "But I'll do it, and can anyone tell me why I'll do it?"

The men in the room replied in unison, "Because Dr. Ego is the most brilliant man on Earth, and soon all the world will be like him."

The man smiled. "Thank you my friends for your confidence and loyalty, which of course you wouldn't give unless they were richly deserved.

"Soon the world will be conformed to our image, but in the meantime we cannot allow an outsider to disseminate concepts that are antithetical to our cause. And yes, I agree it's troubling that we had to engage the services of Dr. Pig, but I assure you that our arrangement will be terminated as soon as we dispense with the present diversion."

Meanwhile, Cur, in his orbit a safe distance above the Earth, assumed that the caller had been simply one more wacko, and fell into a restful sleep.

The following evening, Cur received another call equally as ominous. It had been another long day of trying to make the world a better place, and this time he decided to let his answering machine screen the call.

"Hello, you have reached the orbiting spacecraft of The Mighty Cur. I regret that I am presently unable to take your call, but if you care to leave a message I will endeavor to respond appropriately as soon as possible."

"Cur, it's Sara White. Sorry to bother you at night, but…"

Cur picked up the phone. "Before you say anything else, tell me how many Mobothrakians it takes to change a light bulb."

"None. There's no such thing as a Mobothrakian light bulb because Mobothrakians are self-illuminating."

Cur began to laugh, and then realized that Sara wasn't. He apologized. "Sorry if I sounded abrupt. You would not believe the head-cases out there who have nothing better to do than crank-call an alien super hero."

Sara was clearly upset. "Listen Cur, Dad has a problem. We're not sure what it is, but he insists on seeing you."

Cur of course replied that he would be right there. Sara provided the name and location of the hospital, and in less than a minute Cur's vessel had landed on the roof. He climbed down his rope ladder and knocked on the window of the hospital room.

Rob and Sara ran to the window and let the alien in. As Cur climbed in the window, he accidentally knocked over a plant.

Rob looked around and laughed nervously. "I hate to agree with a low-life like Greed, but isn't there a better way to do this? I mean, haven't any of those super-scientific races you keep talking about found a way to, I don't know, convert people into energy and then have them re-materialize somewhere else?"

Cur began to laugh and then realized that levity was most likely not appropriate under the circumstances. He cleared his throat. "Well, actually you humans are not the only ones to think of that. A race that calls themselves the Borpedeepians did some initial experimentation along the lines that you suggest. However, they were never able to find a way to completely dematerialize complex organisms such as themselves. As a result many Borpedeepians experienced severe headaches as they slammed through walls headfirst traveling from point A to point B. Research finally was terminated."

He paused. "In fact, the expression, 'Well that turned out to be a real Borpedeepian dematerialization of complex life-forms experiment,' became common in certain parts of the galaxy as a short-hand way to describe any endeavor that did not produce planned results."

Rob stared blankly for a moment. "Yeah, right. Listen, why don't you take a look at Sara's dad? He's apparently come down with some sort of viral infection, and the doctors can't figure it out."

Cur approached the bed. Bill put out his hand and weakly took hold of the alien's arm. "They're trying to blame this on you." He whispered.

Cur drew closer. "Bill, you of all people know that's not possible."

Bill spoke again with great effort. "Cur, it doesn't matter. They want to destroy you, no matter what it takes. Nobody has spent more time with you than I have. It's perfect. They can blame my sickness on an alien virus that I contracted from you."

Cur began to stammer. "But, but, why…?"

Mildred broke in, "Because, if you haven't figured it out by now, one of the wonderful aspects of our human nature is that we instinctively hate and mistrust anyone who's different from us—not to mention the fact that there are other agendas at work here. No offense Cur, but right about now

I wish that somebody else had rescued you from those thugs the day you landed."

She began to cry.

Cur was silent for a moment. "Listen, I don't have any technology designed to destroy life, even microscopic life. However, since we do encounter carbon-based life-forms from time to time, I happen to have a device that will bolster Bill's biological functions, which include his internal defense mechanisms."

As Cur began to apply the device, he heard a commotion outside the room. "He's in there officers. The alien is in the room with Mr. Green!"

As several men in uniform entered the room, Rob spun around and blocked their path. He was waving his arms. "Stay back, don't touch it or you'll end up like my father-in-law." The officers hesitated long enough for Cur to finish his procedure.

As they raised their weapons, Cur jumped out of the window, took hold of his rope ladder, and was gone.

One of the officers spoke. "Are you folks all right?"

Bill sat up in bed, appearing markedly better. "Who was that alien?" he quipped. "I never had a chance to thank him."

Sara knelt beside the bed. "Dad, you heard Cur say that he couldn't kill the virus. I don't think we're out of the woods yet. Somebody purposely infected you with an unknown organism just to get him. Until we figure out what's going on, the whole world may be in serious danger."

That evening, Cur sat quietly in the bedroom of his spacecraft attempting to sort out his feelings. He knew that the boost he had given to Bill's internal defenses would revive him temporarily but, like the doctors, he could do nothing to actually cure Bill. He was frustrated over his inability to save his friend.

His brooding was interrupted by the telephone, and he decided to again let the answering machine take the call.

As his caller began to speak, Cur's alien blood ran cold.

"Hello, Cur. I know you're up there and I know you can hear me. I want to meet with you. In return, I will give you the antidote that will cure Bill Green."

Cur grabbed the receiver. "Who is this?"

The caller was obviously pleased that he had gotten through. "My name is Ebenezer Goe, but most people know me as Doctor Ego."

Cur mumbled, "Dr. Ego, huh? Interesting name."

The caller laughed. "Surely my alien friend, someone such as yourself coming from an advanced civilization must realize that there is more than one way to classify people. I, being a superior being, divide people into two categories, me and not me. Now it stands to reason that if I'm to increase, people who are not me need to decrease."

Hearing no response, Ego went on. "Now listen, I just want to meet with you. No tricks, and please, no alien jokes or riddles. You meet with me, and I give you the antidote to Bill Green's unfortunate malady."

Cur was uncertain as to what to do, and so asked simply, "What do you really want?"

Dr. Ego answered warmly, "Why Cur, the same thing you do, to help mankind. I know you have reason to be suspicious, but you have to come out of that box sometime. Besides, I'll tell you what, you can let your vessel hover overhead while we meet in the parking lot of my office. I'll give you the antidote, and if you don't like what I have to say you can just leave. There is absolutely no risk or obligation."

Even Cur, who was still extremely naive by human standards, recognized that this was obviously a trap. However, he also reminded himself of a previous observation that only on a planet such as this could there be real heroes, and sometimes heroes need to walk into traps. Besides, it appeared that he did not have a choice.

"All right Ego, you win. Just give me the location."

Dr. Ego did so, and within seconds saw the Curian spacecraft descend past his office window.

As Cur waited in the parking lot, Doctor Ebenezer Goe emerged from the adjoining office building. He introduced himself and handed Cur a vial, which he said contained the antidote to Bill's disease. "You see, Cur, sometimes even humans keep their word."

Cur remained expressionless. "All right talk, but make it quick. I don't know what you're up to, but I have a friend who desperately needs this."

Dr. Ego was still smiling. "Actually Cur, all I want you to do is listen to a short tape." He pulled out a small cassette player and pressed the start button. Suddenly, Cur felt that strange heaviness that he had experienced occasionally before. This time however, it was overwhelming. As the alien felt himself growing dizzy, three men, each of whom looked as though he could be Dr. Ego's twin, appeared and pushed Cur into a car. As they drove away, Cur's vessel did not react but remained motionless, hovering where Cur had left it.

As the car wound its way through unfamiliar streets, Cur found himself aware of everything that was happening, but somehow unable to react, immobilized by the words and music emanating from Dr. Ego's cassette tape player. Finally they arrived at another impressive office building and pulled into the parking garage.

Still dazed, Cur was handcuffed and pushed into a large auditorium. He felt he must be hallucinating. As Dr. Ego strode towards the podium, hundreds of men, all of them identical in appearance to Dr. Ego, rose to their feet and applauded. He basked in their praise for several minutes, then raised his hand and asked that they be seated.

"My fellow Egomaniacs," he shouted, "we have again proven our intellectual superiority by accomplishing something that has consistently eluded many of the world's governments and institutions. We have done what the combined forces of Greed and Pig were not able to accomplish. We have captured the alien invader known as Cur, and even now he lies helpless in our power, as all of you can plainly see."

The room again exploded into thunderous applause. Cur could not help but notice that not only did everyone in the room look the same, but also they all moved precisely in unison. For the next hour, Dr. Ego rambled on about his own greatness, and at each pause the audience cheered. Finally he asked if there were any questions.

Everyone in the room (with the exception of Cur, of course) raised their hands. They all had the same question: "Why doesn't the world recognize our greatness?"

"Because they're pitiable fools!" Ego screamed, and the audience again clapped and cheered for several minutes. Cur raised his hand and everyone in the audience gasped simultaneously. Goe, motioning for silence, said with a smirking grin, "The chair recognizes the alien prisoner."

Cur still found it difficult to focus as he continued to struggle with unfamiliar thoughts and feelings but managed to get the words out. "I don't mean to sound judgmental, but you really need to re-examine your approach to life. I think I would be remiss if I did not point out the principle that 'a haughty spirit goes before destruction.'"

As one man, Ego and all of his duplicates pointed at Cur and shouted, "Blasphemy!"

Despite the intensity of their outrage, it subsided quickly, and Ego called out to one of his duplicates, "Dr. Ego, would you escort our prisoner to the holding room?" One of the group stepped forward and replied, "Certainly, Dr. Ego," and taking Cur by the arm, he led him out of the auditorium and into a room that appeared comfortable enough, but which had no windows and no doors other than the one by which they had entered.

Cur did not have long to wait before the "real" Ebenezer Goe appeared, wearing a huge triumphant smile. "I'm sure you have a great many questions," he said laughing, "and as I'm sure you know, the bad guys always relish the chance to explain everything to the seemingly helpless hero. Excuse me, to the seemingly helpless super-hero. So go ahead, ask me anything, this is your chance."

"All right," Cur responded weakly, still fighting a battle within, "why do all the villains here have the title 'Doctor'?"

"Not all of us do, just us well-educated madmen." Ego replied, still wearing the plastic smile. "Actually, it was either that or 'Insurance Company,' but two out of three of us voted for 'Doctor.' Next question please."

"I've got to ask, who are all those guys who look exactly like you, and what is their purpose?

Ego's smile grew even larger. "Let me begin with my personal philosophy. I believe that I am the most important person on Earth, and everything in the world centers on me. Consequently, when I formed this organization, I made it a firm rule that in order to join, new members had to be just like me in every respect. Needless to say, it was impossible to find other human beings that came up to that standard. Therefore I created an army of androids, each of which is indistinguishable from myself, unless of course a medical test is performed. That, by the way, is where you come in, but I'm getting ahead of myself."

Cur interrupted. "Excuse me Doctor, but have you ever considered using your intellect and skills for the betterment of others? You know, putting the interests of others ahead of your own."

Ego momentarily lost the plastic smile and sneered. "A well adjusted man never puts others ahead of himself."

The plastic smile reappeared. "The only android that's not me is the one I built for Peaceful Planet. I hated to do that, but frankly I needed the money."

"In any case, our goal is to rule the world, simply because we are the most qualified to do so. That process is well under way in the United States as hundreds of my Egomaniacs have secured positions in government agencies across the country."

Cur interrupted, "I hate to break the news, but the United States is still a democracy. No offense, but who in their right mind would vote for one of your duplicates for anything?"

Goe laughed. "Let me repeat, government *agencies*. The truth is, my good alien, that the real power in this great nation has come to rest not in the elected officials, who are subject to public scrutiny and held accountable for their actions, but in countless people who are not subject to any such pressures and yet wield incredible power over the lives of private citizens.

"If I control the agencies, I can shut down any business, ruin anyone's life, or if it suits my purpose, make someone else, no matter how undeserving, prosper. And no one will ever notice that the man working in San Francisco is the same one working in Denver, is the same one working in Minneapolis, is the same one working in Dallas, etc., etc. Every once in a while, one of my Egomaniacs will encounter some troublesome fellow-employee who insists on doing the right thing, whatever that means, but fortunately there are not many people like that around anymore."

Cur put up his hands. "All right, the big question, what did you do to me, and why didn't my ship come to get me?"

"You'll find out tomorrow. In the meantime, you'll find a generator in the corner of your room that produces a wide range of radiant energy. Good night."

As Ego left the room, Cur began to feel overwhelmed by internal forces he had never experienced prior to coming to Earth, but now had become all too familiar—loneliness and worry.

That night proved to be the longest Cur could remember. And as the android Egos watched their monitors, they noted that the alien spent several hours in that unusual kneeling position which they had not been programmed to comprehend.

Early the next morning, Dr. Ego returned. "Well, I trust you had a good night's sleep."

"Actually, no," Cur replied, still visibly shaken.

"Well, no matter," Ego went on cheerfully, we can proceed with my agenda anyway."

"Your agenda?" Cur muttered.

"Yes, my hopelessly innocent alien. You are about to become the first affiliate member of the Egomaniacs, and I'm going to win you over with nothing more than this little cassette tape player and a couple of very large speakers."

Goe pressed a button on his tape player, and Cur suddenly found himself engulfed by a vile bombardment of bigotry, anger, selfishness, sexual perversion, and lies that far exceeded anything he had yet experienced on Earth.

The alien felt strangely weak and sick. Finding it difficult to think clearly, he begged Ego to stop.

The doctor only laughed more heartily. "What you are hearing was compiled by my associate, Doctor Pig. He has drawn on the worst, or by his reckoning, the best he could find from both historical and current sources. There are excerpts from modern dictators, mass murderers, and purveyors of fear and oppression from all over the world played against a backdrop of the most insidious preaching of hate and perversion to be found in modern music. But, you know what? In this great land of diversity and freedom of expression, Doctor Pig was able to secure funding for this from the National Entitlement for the Arts! Enjoy!"

Cur began to feel not just the heaviness he had experienced earlier, but a wrenching nausea. As he fell to the floor, a burst of radiant energy erupted from every cell in his body. Lapsing into semi-consciousness, he saw again the image of something unspeakably monstrous laughing, which he had seen in Washington when he rescued the woman who was under attack.

Ego continued to gloat. "You know, Cur, this process would take much longer for the average human, who would be somewhat hardened to the kinds of things you're hearing. In fact, I'm sure there are some people out there whom this would not affect at all. Unfortunately for you however, your innocence and naiveté make this not only a rapid process, but also an excruciatingly painful one."

Ego abruptly turned off the recording. "You see Cur, Greed's big mistake was trying to beat you on a physical level. That is not surprising given that his entire focus is on material acquisitions, what some might call the 'lust of the eyes'. Unfortunately for him, that approach was doomed to failure from the start, given the respective levels of our technologies. What I have done is to beat you on a moral and spiritual level. Your ship has not come to your rescue because I have subjected you to the one kind of danger for which you could not possibly have programmed it to respond. There is nothing in the history of your race that could have prepared you for what is happening here today."

Goe's grin grew wider. "You see, my alien friend, I understand completely why you were different prior to coming here, why you were upset that you came, and why you can't go back. And, oh yes, I know all about the things you can't discuss. For perhaps the first time in my life, I'm glad my hypocritical parents drug me to Sunday school when I was a kid. Those poor innocent fools at the church gave me the information I needed to conclude my greatest triumph.

"But take heart. You'll find that once you hear this stuff often enough it won't even bother you any more. The longer you're here, the more complete your transformation will be."

Ego may have been right. Cur was surprised to find that he could actually visualize his hands tightening around his enemy's throat. While one side of him was repulsed at such a thought, there was another side that relished it.

As Ego stood grinning, the alien fought to clear his head. "What do you want from me?"

"I didn't tell you before because I wanted to present this when you were in a proper frame of mind." Ego leaned forward and, as if revealing some grand scheme, declared, "I want you to clone me."

Cur looked at him strangely. "You're going to have to explain this. I hate to tell you Doc, can I call you 'Doc?', but 'clone' is another one of those human words for which I can find no equivalent in any known language."

Ego shook his fist. "Don't get cute with me alien. I've seen what you can do. There's no way a race as advanced as the Curians can't perform a simple cloning."

Seeing Cur's blank expression sent Goe into a rage. "Clone. Clone. You idiot! Clone! Use my DNA to make more of me! It's been done already with sheep and other animals! I've tried to accept these androids as being me, but they're just not good enough. I want more of me. I want me everywhere, running everything, loved by everybody. And if you don't give me that, I'll break you and sell you to Greed."

Ego, breathing heavily, stared at the alien, waiting for some response. Not hearing any, he sneered, "Maybe I'll just unleash my plague on the whole world. Maybe that's how I'll fulfill my dreams of world domination."

Cur stared back, his teeth clenched as he fought back feelings he did not want to feel. "You're insane."

Ego began to shriek, "Insane? Insane? I've heard that before. Well say goodbye to every shred of decency in that wretched alien body."

Ego pressed the play button on his recorder, but nothing happened. He started to pound on it, then heard a voice from the other side of the room. "The game's over, E. Goe, I'm taking the alien back to his ship."

Dr. Goe spun around to see one of his duplicates walking slowly towards him. "Dr. Ego, have you gone mad? What happened to your programming? What has this alien done to you?"

The newly entered Dr. Ego seemed to ignore the angry super-villain and walked towards the alien. "Hello Cur, time to go home." He pulled off a mask, revealing that he was not one of the Egomaniacs at all. In fact, he was someone Cur had met before but couldn't quite place.

The man took Cur's arm in an effort to give him some support. "I know you're bad on names, but I'm Justin Black with the FBI. You know my brother, Jimmy, the environmentalist? He introduced us a while back. I've been assigned to watch you."

Cur managed a smile for the first time in days. "Yes, I like your brother. He turned out to be a pretty nice guy, once he got over a misplaced sense of self-importance."

Ego broke in, "Hey, watch it, around here self-importance is a virtue."

Cur ignored him and continued. "But how, Justin? How did you do this? How did you..."

"Later," Black breathed quickly. "For now, let's just say that people with inflated views of themselves are always easy to outwit."

Ego shouted, "I have no idea what you mean by that, but you're the fool. My fellow Egomaniacs will kill you."

Already, they could hear the sounds of androids approaching. Black looked at Cur grimly. "Forgive me, my friend, for what I am about to do."

He pushed Cur aside, picked up a chair, and with all the strength he could muster, broke it over the alien's back.

Cur howled in pain, "Oooow, hey! That wasn't very nice! Do you mind if I ask what you think you're doing?"

As Cur fell to the floor, Black repeatedly kicked the alien. "I'm subjecting you to a physical attack so that wonderful box of yours can come and save us!"

Cur forced a wry smile. "Thank you, uh, whatever you're name is, but I think maybe by now you've hurt me enough."

Suddenly, a section of the outside wall was pulled away, and Cur could see his vessel through the hole. A familiar mechanical voice announced, "This unit is engaged in the preservation of sentient life. Please stand clear." By this time the android Egos had arrived. Shots were fired, but in vain, as the bullets exploded in mid-air.

The Curian vessel apparently recognized that the androids were non-living. Those that continued to advance were thrown backwards, as if by some invisible hand. Black lifted the alien onto his shoulder and began to ascend the rope ladder with unexpected speed. "Whatever you're made of, its lighter than it looks."

Meanwhile the human Ego stood his ground, apparently unaffected by the alien force that so easily repelled his androids. He was seething with rage. As Justin Black and Cur fell into the spacecraft, he shook his fist and shouted, "The game's not yet played out, alien! We'll meet again, and I'll beat you, even if I have to do the one thing I hate most in all the world—ask for help!"

As Ego continued his self-centered tantrum, the Curian ship vanished. Inside, the alien smiled weakly at his human benefactor. "You know, when we first met in Washington you told me I might escape through a hole in the wall. Did you know something?"

Justin, who was normally one of those people whose expression rarely changed, began to laugh in spite of himself. "Hey, you told me that monitoring your activities would be the easiest job on the planet." He paused. "And when I get home and my wife asks me what I did today, I'll tell her I saved the life of a space alien by beating him with a chair."

Cur stared for a moment, and then for the first time in weeks broke into uncontrollable laughter as the stress of Bill Green's illness and his encounter with Doctor Ego at last found release. He felt his head begin to clear, although his thought-life would not be the same for the next several weeks. The good news was that Cur had apparently made a new friend on this strange planet and again found himself awed by human courage and decency, which always seemed to manifest themselves unexpectedly and in the worst of circumstances. Earth was indeed a world of extremes.

Chapter 12

DECK CHAIRS ON THE TITANIC

Cur dropped Justin Black at FBI headquarters and stayed just long enough to answer a few questions. He promised, however, to e-mail a full report before the end of the day regarding his experiences with Dr. Goe.

His primary concern was, of course, Bill Green. The alien had to know whether he had suffered through his experiences with Dr. Ego for nothing, or if he indeed had secured a genuine antidote to administer to his friend.

Upon reaching the hospital, Cur was distressed to find that it was heavily guarded. "Here we go again," he thought to himself. As he began to descend however, he was pleasantly surprised to find that the troops were there not to stop him, but to ensure his safe passage.

A voice emanated from several speakers placed around the grounds of the hospital. "We've cleared the area Cur, please feel free to land and use the front door."

Cur was gratified that at last he seemed to be gaining acceptance on Earth beyond his initial close circle of friends.

He had been rescued from the Egomaniacs by an agency of the United States government and now found himself welcomed by the United States military. In spite of the hardship he had just endured, Cur began to feel warm and fuzzy all over.

The only thing he could not understand was the music. The same five synthesized musical notes kept playing over and over again. With all of the great music created throughout human history, why would they broadcast such an unimaginative, repetitive melody?

Cur brought his ship down in an area of the hospital grounds that had been cleared for him and descended his rope ladder. He could not help but notice that, not far away, a group of activists was shouting and cursing. Some carried signs proclaiming a human's right to kill aliens. These were kept at a safe distance, however, by National Guard troops, who themselves seemed to be the object of a fair amount of verbal abuse.

The alien counted only about twenty protesters, although on the evening news there appeared to be many more.

He entered the hospital safely and was escorted to Bill's room where he was asked to sign an affidavit accepting full legal responsibility and holding the hospital harmless if the antidote failed.

He looked questioningly at Millie, who said simply, "Please Cur, just sign the stupid thing."

Cur did so, and a doctor administered the antidote.

There was nothing to do now but wait. The hospital staff could not help but notice that Mrs. Green joined Cur for some time beside her husband's bed in that unusual kneeling position he often assumed.

As darkness fell and the vigil continued, Cur leaned over to Millie and whispered, "Is there any way we can get the guys outside to play a different song? The music is driving me nuts."

The alien's request was quickly relayed to the proper authorities and, in short order, the computer-generated sequence of tones was replaced with a trombone ensemble playing Beethoven's "Moonlight Sonata." Cur thanked the hospital staff for their intervention and exclaimed, "Now that's what I call music!"

Thankfully, Dr. Ego was concerned enough about his own reputation that the antidote proved to be indeed genuine. Within hours Bill began to show signs of recovery.

Cur stood up, raised his arms, and said, "Praise God!" Everyone in the room immediately went silent and stared in disbelief. One nurse dropped a clipboard.

Millie put her arm around the alien and explained softly, "There are certain expressions that have been officially approved as things you're allowed to say when you're, uh, happy about something. That's not one of them."

Cur simply smiled a tired smile and asked to be excused. He had been through a tremendous ordeal and needed to recover. Besides, he had promised the FBI a full report on his experiences with Dr. Ego and was already agonizing over the wording of certain sections. Although as noted earlier, the Curians have a passion for accuracy in written communications, he still found it difficult to say anything derogatory about anyone, even a man who had attempted to destroy him.

As he walked out of the hospital and toward his spacecraft, one of the guardsmen remarked, "You know, I don't think that alien's as bad as everybody says he is. I'm not saying I'd have him in my house, but I might go bowling with him."

Cur stopped short, walked over to the man and handed him a piece of paper with his phone number. "Hey, I've never been bowling, but it appears to be a fascinating sport. Let me know when, and I'll be there."

The man was stunned, but Cur went on. "Now look, I get a lot of crank calls, so you need to know the password. I'll ask, 'what do you call a Fraponian zookeeper who visits the Orion Nebula?' and you say, 'a Muepidian who wears funny hats.' Got it?"

The man was speechless. "Uh, actually, uh…"

Cur laughed. "It's a little complicated. I'll explain it when you call. Just remember 'Muepidian who wears funny hats.' Oh, and listen, Tuesday is my best day. Mondays, Wednesdays, and Thursdays I help out with UN relief efforts. Fridays are normally not bad, but I promised the Russians I'd take a look at a malfunctioning space station. Saturday I'm lecturing in Buenos Aires. But seriously, give me a call."

He ascended his rope ladder and almost instantaneously vanished from sight.

It might be noted that in spite of the guardsman's best efforts to convince his family and friends to the contrary, nobody believed that he actually had a tentative date to go bowling with an alien. Eventually, tired of being ridiculed, he decided it was best to drop the subject. Besides, he couldn't remember the joke.

During the next several weeks, Bill Green continued to gain strength, but the family heard almost nothing from Cur.

Meanwhile, public opinion regarding the alien remained volatile. There were some that held tenaciously to the belief that an alien who seemed determined to do nothing but help people in need was not to be feared. Those were normally portrayed however as dangerous reactionaries who threatened the purity of prescribed thought patterns.

That only hurt and confused the alien, who soon found he needed, more than anything else, the refuge of friends. There was no question, of course, as to who he hoped would fill that need.

When the call came, Bill and Millie were ecstatic to hear from him again. They arranged another clandestine meeting, this time for reasons of safety, in a somewhat remote region of Canada. On top of everything else, the Greens were finding that their friendship with Cur was resulting in increasing hostility from their friends and neighbors.

Unfortunately, in spite of his best efforts to be simply a nice guy trying to do the right thing, Cur was still repeatedly vilified in the newspapers and on the nightly news. Apparently, the money spent to promote "The Cur Song" was still paying dividends. The result was a continued shift in public attitudes, even among people who staunchly maintained that they were not influenced by the media.

In addition, slanderous attacks seemed to be coming from other directions and in a variety of forms. Cur was ridiculed in certain comic strips as part of the long-standing assault on "traditional" values that dated back to the latter part of the twentieth-century. He was also the brunt of repetitious uncomplimentary comments by fictitious characters on certain television shows, which, inexplicably, many people found humorous.

Nevertheless, as public opinion in general moved toward greater fear and mistrust of the alien, Cur's friends and supporters became more fiercely loyal. Again however, life was not always easy for those courageous individuals. They increasingly found themselves labeled as "alienists," a term that eventually came to be applied to anyone who became the target of any kind of verbal attack of any nature.

For the moment though, Cur was willing to let the social engineers and opinion makers have their day at his expense. For now, he was happy to have the company and counsel of his trusted friends.

Bill lit a fire in the cabin they had rented and promised his alien friend that he would not try to trick him into saying anything he wasn't supposed to say.

Cur was appreciative. "You know Bill, sometimes I get so angry and confused that it would not take much for me to break all the rules. I finally understand what a powerful force temptation is for those humans who wish to do right."

Millie entered the room. "It's a good thing we possess a power beyond ourselves."

Cur looked at her thoughtfully. "Do you mean...?"

Millie put up her hands. "Oops, sorry. There are certain things I'm not permitted to discuss with Curians."

Cur was stunned at first. Then abruptly his expression changed and he laughed out loud. "You got me! Please forgive me my friends, I can't believe how tense and uptight I've become."

Cur had always appreciated the positive effects of laughter, but now in the context of the trials he had endured, it seemed at the moment to be particularly therapeutic.

He went on to unburden himself to the Greens. He spoke of the unwanted attitudes and feelings that seemed to be gaining a firmer and firmer grip on his soul. He confessed his bitterness, malice, hunger for revenge, racism, and immoral thoughts. He found himself struggling with things, which in his former life were not only unknown, but also unthinkable.

While it was painful to admit those things, Cur found a strange peace resulted from doing so. Finally he asked, "Bill, Millie, is this what it's like to be human? Does everyone on Earth have this battle raging within themselves?"

Bill replied slowly, "Cur, first let me say that everyone here is subject to the things you described. However, not everyone fights them or goes to the proper source for power. Most people, sad to say, actually enjoy the things you mentioned and even take pride in acting them out."

Cur shook his head. "That makes absolutely no sense, but explains a lot of what I've seen."

As the day wore on, Cur began to feel like himself again. That afternoon the three went hiking. When night fell, Cur retrieved a long-range scanner from his ship. It was a surprisingly compact device that included an optical telescope as well as a number of other instruments whose function the Greens could not quite grasp. The stars were beautiful, and as the hours passed, they found themselves spellbound listening to an astronomy lesson taught by someone who had actually visited many of the objects they examined.

As the drop in temperature became more noticeable, the trio decided to return to the cabin. At that moment however, a light on the Curian device began to flash, and something like an alarm bell began to sound. Millie started to make a wisecrack, then noticed that Cur's expression was grim. "We've got a problem, I...I mean a situation that requires attention," he stuttered.

Bill and Millie found themselves alarmed by Cur's tone of voice. "What do you mean, a situation?" Bill demanded. "What's going on?"

"Stay with me another minute," Cur replied quickly, without looking up. "Let me just be sure I have this right."

"Have what right?" Bill snapped, showing uncharacteristic impatience.

Cur did not respond, but kept working his instruments.

Millie took her husband's arm. "C'mon Bill, you're beginning to sound like you did that day in the New York motel room. Give the guy a chance."

Bill again demanded an explanation, but once again an answer was not forthcoming. "Is this another one of those things you're going to get all upset about, but can't discuss?"

Finally Cur lifted his head. "There's a comet on a collision course with your world. It will strike Earth in 179 days, causing incalculable damage, and ultimately destroying between 85% and 90% of all life here. If I had a Klucktonian xaxomatic infrared energy reader with me, I could perform more accurate calculations, but…"

"Are you serious?" Bill shouted. "This isn't the start of one of your Curian stories, is it? You know, we have people who watch for these things too. Why haven't they picked this up?"

"Because it's not a known object and it's much too distant," Cur answered quietly. "Besides, you might recall that on March 23, 1989 a comet a half mile in diameter crossed Earth's orbit and came within 700,000 miles of the Earth. No human observer saw it coming. If it had arrived at that point just six hours later, it would have produced the same kind of unexpected cataclysm."

"We've come a long way since 1989," Bill mumbled.

Cur ignored him and continued his explanation. "This particular object is not even in orbit around the sun. It's what we call a drifter, possibly the result of some ancient super-nova or other explosion. It's approaching the solar system from outside our galaxy at an angle almost perpendicular to Earth's orbit. Your astronomers will detect it, but again, not in time to stop it."

"Stop it?" Millie broke in. "Back up a second. You said 'not in time to stop it,' so that says to me that if we do something in time, it *can* be stopped, right?"

Cur gazed into the sky. "Yes, but…" He paused.

"But what?" Bill was shouting again. "We're talking about the end of the world, and I feel like I'm pulling teeth!"

"I can't do it."

Bill threw up his hands. "I know, I know. You have some sort of primary imperative or something that prohibits you from interfering in the natural evolution of human history."

"Uh, no. Where did you come up with that? No, actually, if I was traveling in something larger than a shuttlecraft and was permitted beyond the orbit of Earth's moon, I could take care of this myself. But by the time the comet gets that close, its speed, amplified by Earth's gravitational pull, will be too much for the limited instrumentation on my ship to make much of a difference."

Bill still appeared to be agitated. "Wait a minute. You're always telling us about all these different races of beings flying around out there. Isn't it likely that one of them will spot what's happening and do something about it?"

Cur sighed. "Bill, under normal circumstances you would be right." He paused as if to gather his thoughts. "But given that, number one, I was somehow forced to land here, a forbidden planet, and then, number two, the Curian fleet received a threatening communication from Earth, I can't imagine that anybody's going to come within ten light years of this place for quite a long time."

"So the bottom line," Bill concluded, "is that *we* have to stop it."

"Yes, that's what I'm trying to say," Cur replied, gazing intently at his human friends. "The good news is that the human race has the technology to avert this crisis. If your national leaders will listen to me, the comet can be diverted by two or at the most three nuclear missiles. I, of course, can provide the precise coordinates and level of necessary firepower once the comet is a little closer."

For a moment there was silence. Then Millie, who was jumping up and down and rubbing her arms, said dryly, "If you gentlemen don't mind, could we save the world from inside where it's warm?"

The conversation inside the cabin was brief, as there seemed to be only one logical course of action. They would leave the car and all three would immediately fly to Washington D.C. in the Curian ship, praying for receptive ears at the highest levels of power.

As they approached the nation's capital, Cur attempted to radio the White House. This was a call the administration did not want to receive, especially in an election year. After all, what politician in his right mind would launch nuclear missiles at an unseen target on the advice of a non-human who was so hated by current opinion-makers? Cur was informed that he could be penciled in to meet with administration aides in about five or six months.

Somewhat frustrated, Cur called General Brown's private line, confident that at least the general would listen to what he had to say. The general's private secretary informed him that the general had died suddenly just a few days before. Cur immediately felt himself overwhelmed by another new emotion—grief. The Greens could not help but notice however, that Cur appeared strangely at peace towards the conclusion of the conversation.

"What was that all about?" Bill asked.

Cur again appeared frustrated. "The general just died. I'll explain the rest later. Right now, you have to tell me how to get the message out. You're the humans here, tell me how to communicate to the people of this planet that their destruction is imminent."

"Why don't you make another television appearance?" Millie offered. "Everybody accepts what they see on TV."

Cur was thoughtful. "You know, I got in a lot of trouble with the network sponsors for doing that before. If I do it again, what do you think I should say?"

"Believe the message and divert the comet, or die."

Cur was silent for a moment. "That sounds awfully blunt. Isn't there a more, you know, diplomatic way to say it?"

Bill and Millie just stared, and the alien shrugged. "All right, let's give it a try."

And once again television viewing across the country was interrupted by an unexpected special announcement.

"Hi, my name is Cur and these are my friends, Bill and Millie Green."

Bill and Millie smiled awkwardly and waved.

"Listen, I hate to interrupt what you're watching, but I just thought you ought to know that there's a comet on a collision course with Earth. If it's not stopped or diverted it will strike the Earth 178 days from now, causing unimaginable death, destruction, and suffering. Please contact your elected officials and tell them that you support the launching of nuclear missiles to alter its course and save the world. I apologize again for this discourteous interruption, but I thought you ought to know about your impending doom. Thank you, have a nice night and a great day tomorrow."

Cur turned to his friends. "How do you think it went?"

"Well," Bill suggested, "let's put the TV on and find out."

Each of the major networks plus several local stations appeared on the Curian monitor mounted on the far wall of the ship. It soon became apparent that Cur's announcement did not produce its intended result.

The message was delivered the evening before Halloween, and many viewers assumed that the announcement was for entertainment purposes only.

It also came during the final seconds of a football game, and so in many average American households, people were livid that they had to miss the end of the game just so some alien could give them the date the world would end.

A few networks decided to stop people on the street and ask them what they thought.

Typical comments included:

> A BUSINESSPERSON: Look, I've got two jobs and I'm trying to raise a family. I don't have time to worry about the destruction of humanity.
> AN ACTIVIST: This is obviously an issue of race and gender, and I'm outraged.
> AMERICAN TEENAGER: I intend to live the rest of my life to the fullest, and I'm starting by hanging out at the convenience store.
> A MOVIE BUFF: Cur's obviously been watching too many disaster flicks from the 90's.
> MOST PEOPLE: Cur is the guy in the song. The song says he's bad. He must be wrong.
> ANONYMOUS: Huh?

However, not all was lost. The next morning, Cur received a call from the host of a daytime TV talk show who asked him to appear as a special guest. Not long after this, he was contacted by a post-secondary school in the northeastern part of the country and was invited to debate one of the faculty.

The alien was encouraged. Finally it appeared people were at least willing to listen.

During the next few days, Cur embarked on a unique new strategy. He took to the streets with a microphone and boxes of pamphlets explaining the coming catastrophe and how it might be avoided. He was determined to get the message out. Sometimes he spoke on street corners and sometimes he approached people individually.

There were always a few who would listen and, while not always immediately accepting what he had to say, would ask thoughtful questions. Most, however, tried to ignore him, took the pamphlet and kept walking, or responded with something like, "Thank you, but I have my own religion."

The morning of Cur's scheduled appearance on the TV talk show, he decided to impress the audience and appear in his official Curian Space Patrol dress uniform. Bill and Millie, however, asked him as tactfully as they could to change into something that did not so closely resemble an olive-green leisure suit.

Based on prior experience, Cur was understandably cautious regarding this particular forum. Nevertheless, the show seemed to begin innocently enough. There was music and, it seemed to the alien, excessive clapping. His host asked a few non-controversial questions about the customs and culture of his home world. The topic of conversation moved very quickly, however, to the approaching comet.

> INTERVIEWER: Tell our audience about this comet. What makes you think, number one it's there, and number two, it's going to hit us?

CUR: Actually, I discovered it accidentally while examining other astronomical objects that lay in the same general direction. It is presently not detectable by Earthian instruments due to its size and distance. Now, in answer to your second question, I happened to have a Frumpian space-time directional simulator connected to my long-range scanning equipment. You see, the Frumpians are masters at measuring not only the spatial position, direction, and velocity of any given object, but also the influence on its physical movement brought about by other astronomical objects. The Frumpians have taken the further step of programming their instrumentation to automatically alert its users of anything significant that, unless some intervention takes place, will occur in the near future. Unfortunately, I don't have a Klucktonian xaxomatic low-level energy reader with me or I could calculate precisely the time and point of impact.

Now, let me try to explain how this works. As you know, visible light forms only a small portion of the total spectrum of electromagnetic radiation. And while not all objects in the universe emit visible light, every object composed of what we call B-type matter, and not at a temperature of absolute zero, radiates photons at various wavelengths and frequencies. At any given temperature, any object radiates primarily within a certain band of...

INTERVIEWER: Please Cur, you're putting us to sleep. If you can't answer a question in less than three sentences, our viewers are just not interested. (Then facing the camera) We'll be back, right after these messages.

While home viewers watched a sincere-looking man explain how he could help them turn physical harm to their personal advantage by milking their insurance company, Cur received some friendly coaching from his host. Soon they were back on the air.

> INTERVIEWER: Cur, you mentioned two other alien races, which you called the Frumpians and the Klucktonians. Who are they, and what can you tell us about them, briefly, that may be entertaining to our audience?
>
> CUR: Well, let's see. Like the Curians and yourselves, both are tripartite beings composed of a physical body, a soul, and a spirit. The Frumpians do very little actual space-travel, preferring to study the universe from home. When the Curians first encountered them, it became immediately apparent why they don't get out much. You see, their culture elevates the pursuit of logic and demands denial of emotional feelings. As a result, they're really, really, (he paused for effect) booorrrring!
>
> Let me tell you, it's really tough to spend much time with a Frumpian and not begin to feel drowsy. And get this, any time anybody shows a little emotion about anything, they lapse into these monotonous lectures about logic! I mean, give me a break! The Curians are just as anxious as anyone to expand the frontiers of knowledge, but we also like to enjoy ourselves while we're doing it. Anyway, what the Frumpians lack in personality, they make up with mental acumen. They're brilliant students of spatial dynamics, and the Curians have learned a great deal from them.

The Curians also had a difficult time initially with the Klucktonians, but in this case there was a barrier of another kind to overcome. You see each Klucktonian is about the size of, would you believe, the state of Rhode Island, and we had to build these huge amplifiers just to be able to talk to them. (Cur stood up with his arms extended) I mean, what a project!

And then, because they were really big, we kind of expected them to be, you know, a little slow on the draw mentally. Boy, were we wrong! Like the Frumpians, they are exceptional scientists, especially in the area of...

INTERVIEWER: Cur, I'm sorry for interrupting, but we're getting too much light here and not enough heat. Let me try this from a different angle. Cur, I'm sure you realize that you've gotten a lot of people upset by all this talk about a collision between Earth and another astronomical body. Excuse me for being blunt, but how can you be so narrow minded and insensitive? Don't you realize the mental anguish you're causing? Besides, what right do you have to impose your beliefs on others?

The applause light went on and most of the audience either cheered or waved their fists in the air while making ape-like vocal sounds.

CUR: I'm not sure how I should answer that. Every civilization the Curians have ever encountered, except this one, accepts the basic tenet that feelings must be subordinated to truth. Whether or not anyone likes the idea, the fact remains that a comet will collide with this planet in 159 days, unless mankind stops it.

The show's host invited members of the audience to respond.

> GUEST 1 (female): Would you please refrain from the use of "mankind." I find that # * #! expression extremely offensive.
> CUR: Sorry.
> GUEST 2: All this talk about an approaching comet offends me, and if it offends me, you shouldn't be allowed to say it.
> CUR: Isn't it preferable to be offended and live, than to not be offended and die?
> GUEST 3: Everybody knows about the "groupies" who follow you wherever you go. Have you ever gone to bed with a human female?

Cur was silent for a moment, but found that he could not completely contain his anger.

> CUR: This time I'm the one who is offended and find myself again shocked at the depths of depravity to which your race has fallen. Unlike humans, Curians marry for life and remain faithful to their spouses, and even if I was tempted in that area, under no circumstances would I even remotely consider intimacy with someone of another species.
> GUEST 4: Cur, you're wrong about one thing. In spite of what you may have been led to believe, there are still many people on Earth committed to sexual pu-

rity and marital fidelity. The voices you hear do not speak for everybody.

Interviewer (aside): Who let that guy in?

Interviewer: I have a question, Cur. Numerous times you've made reference to other space-traveling races. Why can't the Curians or one of those other technologically advanced species help us out and move the comet for us? Why do we have to drag our own military into this?

Cur's answer came slowly and, it appeared, painfully. "Any one of them would be glad to help, but unless my instruments are just not detecting somebody, no physical beings but us are anywhere near here. I hate to say it, but your only solution to this crisis is to believe me. To put it as simply as I can, your choice is believe or perish."

The audience grew quiet. Cur's host leaned forward and said, "Wait a minute. I think I'm on to something here. You've been quoted before as saying that you think you have a reason for being here, some sort of mission. Whose reason? Whose mission?"

Cur began to say something, but was cut off.

"Don't interrupt me. This is my show. Now, is it possible you're saying that someone sent you here to warn the world?"

Cur hesitated, looked as though he was about to reply and then changed his mind, responding instead, "If I told you, you would never believe me."

Members of the audience demanded to know who it was. Who would have the audacity to send a messenger to warn the world of impending destruction and then hold the world accountable for its response? Just before another commercial break, the camera focused on several rows of people, arm in arm, singing the Cur Song.

> "Cur has got to be destroyed.
> Cur has got to be eliminated.
> He's an enemy of this world.
> The alien must be exterminated."

Most saw that as a heart-warming display of human unity.

Just as the camera swung back towards the stage, someone ran out from behind the curtain and threw a tray of food on the alien.

Chapter 13

ALL THAT IS IN THE WORLD

IN THE DAYS FOLLOWING his television talk show appearance, Cur struggled with feelings of loneliness and despair to a greater degree than he had at any time since his arrival on Earth. It wasn't so much the responses he was receiving to his message. He had grown accustomed to irrationality. It was more the nagging fear that he would die a senseless death with the humans, one death among billions that could easily have been prevented.

Cur's visit to the university did not go well either. He was encouraged by the large crowd that had gathered to hear him, but only minutes into his presentation the meeting was disrupted by SAS (Students Against Sensorship [sic]), who continued to shout and chant until he was forced to suspend his remarks.

The professor who agreed to debate him took the microphone. To the cheers of many of those gathered, he enumerated various reasons why he was opposed to a comet striking the Earth.

When Cur's chance came to respond, he did so quickly, hoping to avoid being cut off again. Speaking as rapidly as he could, he managed to blurt out, "Every civilization the Curians have ever encountered, except this one, accepts the basic tenet that feelings must be subordinated to truth. Whether or not anyone likes the idea, the fact remains that a comet will collide with this planet in 140 days, unless mankind stops it."

The professor sighed, "You're mistaken Cur, people on Earth do care about truth. It's just that we've come to understand that truth is relative. What's truth for you may not be truth for me. You've been saying that there's a comet out there on an intercept course with Earth. Even if people choose not to believe it, you still have to respect them."

Cur was visibly irritated. "This has nothing to do with respect, I'm just trying to warn the world about..."

The professor continued. "Besides Cur, even assuming you're right, what you're saying still doesn't make any sense. No comet that we've ever encountered could cause the kind of damage you describe. Can you elaborate in terms our students can understand?"

Cur spoke as quickly as he could and attempted to comply with the professor's request. "It's a very big comet and it's moving very fast."

He could not continue. The protesters were causing such a commotion that the debate was postponed. Both parties agreed that it would be held at some point in the future in another country—hopefully, in the not too distant future.

It was becoming more and more apparent that the only way Cur was ever going to get the message out was by taking it to the streets. He again began to travel from city to city speaking on street corners or anywhere he could find people willing to listen.

During the summer months he was encouraged to find many churches who offered to have him appear as a guest speaker, particularly in light of the fact that he had no use for human currency and so did not require an honorarium. Most of the churches where he spoke loved his message and told him how blessed they were by what he had to say. The government's inaction and the biased reporting by the liberal media outraged them.

Unfortunately, few church members were willing to actually do something, even if that something was simply to write letters to their elected officials. Those few who really were motivated to take action found their time so hopelessly consumed by committee meetings that they were able to accomplish very little on a practical level.

Cur meanwhile was becoming more and more frustrated by his lack of progress and the seeming inability of this strange race of people to be honest about their true condition and to pursue a course of action to save themselves.

Nevertheless, he determined to continue his crusade because, as everyone in the rest of the universe knows, truth, once discovered, must never be compromised. He could not have suspected that his efforts to save the world were about to come to an abrupt conclusion.

It was at one of his impromptu public meetings, with the comet only weeks from impact, that Cur spotted a familiar face in the crowd. It was Greed. At the sight of his old enemy, Cur could not continue speaking. Remembering his last encounter with Greed operatives, he found himself overcome with fear.

Greed approached, smiling broadly. "Hello, Cur. Well, today's the day. As you know, I've devoted a substantial sum of money to your destruction and I'm finally about to cash in on my investment."

Cur began to ask what good Greed's money would be to him if he, along with the rest of the world, died as a result of the comet. The alien's question was cut short as Greed only laughed sarcastically and was joined by a second man, who Cur recognized from photos as Dr. Pig.

Pig smiled politely at the alien. "My friend, at last we meet face to face. I'm awfully sorry, but I've had to align myself with Greed because, well, there's that outside chance that you could undo centuries of progress. Regrettably, people who would never listen to another human being speak about morality, righteousness, and personal accountability just might be swayed by an alien with a message from the stars. I'm sorry you have to die, but, as you know, it is a foundational tenet of my faith that nobody's life but mine has value."

Cur found it difficult to look directly at Pig as he spoke, and so his eyes wandered across the growing crowd of onlookers. Pig went on, apparently enjoying the sound of his own voice. "With you gone, we can move closer to an ideal world. Imagine, no heaven, no hell, nothing to live or die for. Everybody can just do what feels right and have a good time doing it because nothing matters! You see Cur, I just can't let you ruin our hope for the future."

Cur was beginning to lose his temper. "Ruin what, Dr. Pig? I see people in Greed uniforms everywhere, but I see none of your followers! Where are they?"

Pig laughed repulsively. "You don't get it. Pigs don't contribute. Pigs only gratify themselves!"

As he looked around, Cur, to his horror, spotted several Dr. Egos. *As if things aren't bad enough*, he thought to himself. One of them emerged from the crowd to join Greed and Pig.

Dr. Ego wore the same phony smile that Cur had found so obnoxious during their encounter almost a year ago. "We meet again, alien. I regret having to compromise my principles in joining Pig and Greed, but one must do what one must. The existence of an intellectually advanced alien is too great a threat to my own self- importance."

Cur was dumbfounded. As he considered how to properly respond to such (in his opinion) utter lunacy, his three enemies backed away.

Cur could not recall having seen news cameras up until this point, but they suddenly appeared on all sides. It was to these that Pig, Greed, and Ego directed their attention. As the cameras converged, Pig began to speak. "Fellow citizens of Earth, today we usher in a new age of peace and prosperity to be enjoyed by all the people of this world, as we at last rid our world of the blight of alien influence.

"Of course, no one is truly worthy to be the instrument by which this is accomplished, except possibly Dr. Ego, who insists that he's worthy. But speaking personally, I feel especially honored to play a small role in this great leap forward for mankind. I will be assisted in the destruction of this alien threat by my esteemed colleagues, Doctors Ego and Greed, for we have found that only by working together can we each ultimately succeed."

Cur continued to stand speechless trying to fight the swelling rage he felt within, while the humans who had gathered appeared to be mesmerized by Pig's words.

Abruptly, Dr. Ego signaled with his hand. Several of his duplicate androids approached holding small television sets. Cur began to panic. He knew from first-hand experience the unbridled evil that poured from Ego's tape players and could only imagine what he was about to endure.

Almost simultaneously, several men and women wearing Greed organization uniforms approached with automatic weapons raised. Cur could not help but notice that Greed had assembled his highest-ranking officers—those with a value greater than 90 cents. Most people not directly aligned with one of the three "doctors" began to move away, but a few actually moved closer to the alien. Greed had hoped that the alien would be completely isolated, to ensure that he would avoid any costs of litigation, which would assuredly result if innocent bystanders happened to be caught in the cross fire. Once again he found himself both mystified and irritated by people willing to put themselves at risk in order to do what was right.

Meanwhile, a shadow began to fall as the Curian spacecraft descended and blocked the noonday sun. Cur, quite understandably, called it down as a necessary precaution. As it drew closer, the noise and confusion which had prevailed up to this point evaporated into silence.

Ego laughed maliciously. "Dr. Egos," he shouted. "Ignore that thing. It won't respond to the television attack and besides, its alien programming won't let it hurt anybody anyway."

Instantly and in unison, the Egomaniacs turned on their TVs and an awesome barrage of mind-numbing trash and perversion filled the air. Pig was ecstatic. "This is better than late-night!"

The programming was exactly what Cur expected. What surprised him was that it did not affect him as it had before. He found the broadcast to be revolting, but it did not have the debilitating impact that Ego's tapes had during their first encounter.

Ego was enraged. He screamed at Pig, "What's wrong? What's wrong? You told me this would be more effective than the tape because it added a visual element. If that's the case, why is that abominable alien just standing there? Shouldn't he at least be on his knees?"

Pig scowled, "This is my best work."

Cur focused his gaze on Ego. "You told me I would find that once I was exposed to this stuff often enough it would not even bother me any more. Congratulations, Dr. Goe, you were right. And now, let me show you something else I've learned here on Earth."

If Cur pushed a button or gave a signal, it was certainly not evident to those standing nearby, but immediately bolts of energy flashed in all directions from his ship, shattering each of the television sets held by the Ego androids.

"You know, I used to be utterly opposed to the destruction of property belonging to others, but I've come to understand that on Earth one must always be flexible. Of course, I had to reprogram the instrumentation on my ship to enable it to do what it just did, but as they say, 'when on Earth…'"

Ego, now appearing very insecure, began to back off. Greed, meanwhile, muttered under his breath, "You'd think by now I would have learned never to hire egomaniacs." He raised his arm and shouted, "Open fire! Maybe some shots will get through. And keep firing until there's nothing left. Don't give that thing a chance to regenerate."

For a moment in time, the entire world seemed to explode. Feeling the searing pain of the bullets that ripped through his body, Cur wondered why his ship was so slow to respond. As he fell to the ground, it became clear that he had committed a critical error. In reprogramming the ship's defense systems to allow for offensive action, he had caused a malfunction. Now, tragically, it appeared certain that he had failed. Greed, Pig, and Ego had won, and most life on Earth would end.

And then suddenly, inexplicably to the alien, there was silence.

Apparently, several people in the crowd had thrown themselves into the line of fire. Among them, Cur recognized two of his human friends, Jim and Justin Black. Forgetting for a moment his own physical pain, he knelt beside the bodies and began to cry.

Greed, realizing that humans had been shot, ordered the firing to stop, but turning his face from the cameras, he was crimson with rage. He muttered to himself, "These idiot journalists are liable to say that I'm responsible for the deaths."

Then, turning back to the cameras, he forced himself to appear as sincere as possible. "Those of us in the Greed organization are proud to have fought side by side with the brave men and women who gave up their own lives so unselfishly in the struggle against the alien menace. I hereby authorize a contribution of one million dollars to the families of each of the deceased from the Greed Benevolent Fund. I know it seems like a small gesture at such a time of…"

Greed's remarks were cut short by an angry feminine voice that seemed to come from nowhere and yet everywhere at once, "Would everybody please move out of the way!"

At first nobody moved, and the voice, this time with slightly higher volume and pitch, shouted, "Hello, anybody home? I said, get out of the way!"

As if the day had not held enough surprises, another alien vessel appeared in the sky.

Chapter 14

'TIL DEATH DO US PART

As the spacecraft descended, it became evident that it was similar to Cur's in size and shape, but was beautifully decorated with pastoral scenes. On one side was what appeared to be a bumper sticker which read, "My Daughter is an Honor Student at the Curian Institute for the Research and Analysis of Macro-Cosmic Phenomena." (Note: Curian bumper stickers reformat themselves to conform to indigenous languages).

It landed softly by the scene of the carnage. From the top of the "box" a creature emerged who appeared almost human, except for her nose, which was roughly the size of a watermelon and protruded from the back of her head. She wore a loosely fitting flannel shirt and a pair of battered jeans.

She threw down a rope ladder. As the crowd watched in stunned silence she barked, "What are you people staring at? Didn't I get this right? Isn't this the customary garb worn on this part of your planet?"

She descended the ladder and advanced towards Greed, her face crimson with rage. She raised an alien device and pointed it in his direction, then simply stared as Greed, along with several Egomaniacs, was taken into custody by the police. Pig had vanished.

She turned and walked towards Cur.

He appeared grim. "What do you think you're doing here? Do you have any concept of the ramifications of your decision to come to this planet?"

The visitor flashed a wry smile. "Nice to see you too. In case you're interested, I have a Popolupian Cell Regenerator enhanced by the Spirofoopazoids for use with both modified matter and carbon-based Type B life-forms."

Cur held up his hand and said softly, "Use it on the Earth-people first."

After several minutes, she turned back to Cur, "It appears I was just in time. Some are in pretty bad shape, but they're alive."

In spite of her initial grandstanding, the female alien was visibly shaken and began to weep openly. Summoning what was left of his strength; Cur took her in his arms. "You've never seen anything like this, have you? Well, now that you're here, you might as well know, you're going to see a great deal of pain and even death, but you will never get used to it."

Just then, another commanding voice rang out, "Could everybody hold it for just a minute? We really need to take a commercial break."

Before Cur could respond, the alien woman turned and grabbed the tie of the man who was speaking. "This has not been a good day for me, and if I hear one more word out of you, I'm going to smash this camera over your fat little…" She quickly stopped herself and turned to Cur, blushing.

Cur stared at her for a moment, as if he could not believe what he just saw, then said quietly, "I see you've been infected too."

She shrugged, "You know I couldn't have actually hurt him with my ship so close by. Even on Earth, it wouldn't have let me."

Cur turned and faced the cameras, and with a sweep of his arm, announced, "Ladies and gentlemen of the world, allow me to introduce my wife."

The crowd cheered wildly. Reporters descended upon the pair from every direction. Mrs. Cur, meanwhile, kept tapping her head and repeating, "Log entry, Curian universal memory, next available number please."

The male Cur took his wife's arm. "I think you'll find that we no longer have access."

She appeared a little taken back, "Then how are we supposed to remember things after our brain's physical capacity is used up?"

Her husband did not get a chance to answer. Apparently, although the male Curian had a difficult time finding acceptance on this world, the female Curian, at least for now, found herself instantly popular.

"What do we call you?"

"Cur or 'Hey you in the flannel shirt' will be fine."

"How long has it been since you've seen each other?"

"Well, roughly seventy-five Earth years for me and about fifty for him."

Noting the looks of confusion on the faces around her, she turned to her husband. "Do these guys know about relativity?"

Cur nodded, "In fact, they apply it to everything."

The female Curian paused momentarily. "Okay, whatever, anyway, since we travel at near-light speeds, time for us has been relative."

The male Cur interjected, "Actually fifty-one years two months and seventeen days."

Someone shouted, "Is your ship the same as your husband's? And why is it decorated?"

She laughed. "Well, you know, among the Curians, it's a gender thing. The men generally just want something that will get them from point A to point B. The women want to make a nice appearance as well.

"Why is your nose on the back of your head and your husband's is on the front?"

"Now you're getting personal. We were created this way to facilitate communication and intimacy. As you might imagine, it would be hard to be romantic if both males and females had these big noses..."

"Tell us about your daughter."

She hesitated momentarily and then glanced at her ship. "Oh, the sticker. Well, we're very proud of our daughter, but I probably ought to take that thing off. Unless she's been traveling at near-light speed like we've been for a while, she's got to be over 400 years old by now."

"Actually, we have eighty-two other children. It's amazing, each one of them is different. Would anyone like to see pictures?"

The male Cur broke in, "excuse me Hon, but there's still this little matter of a comet that's about to bring an end to human civilization, and us along with it."

The female Cur smiled. "I'm way ahead of you, goodlookin. On the way in, I spoke to the Russians, and they're taking care of it. If you watch the 6:00 news, you'll see footage of the launchings."

The male Cur was stunned. "Wait a minute. Back up. How did you come to talk to the Russians?"

His wife shrugged. "Actually, I'm not sure. I thought I was supposed to land in New Mexico, but for some reason my ship touched down near a little village called Rasvel."

The male Cur appeared almost human as he gestured with his hands. "Okay, I can accept your landing in Russia. I've experienced a few technical glitches myself. What I can't understand is how, after all I've been through and ended up nowhere, you just land your ship, talk to the humans in Russia, and they believe you?"

His wife shrugged again, "You know how it is, some people are better with first-contact situations than others."

Cur (the male) appeared almost annoyed. "Now wait just a minute!"

His wife laughed, "What did you do, start out by telling them that story about the three sentient beings in the boat?" She watched his expression. "Oh no! You didn't." She laughed almost hysterically, but quickly regained control.

"I'm sorry, I shouldn't make fun. Besides, you've been here much longer than I have, so you must have noticed that the message sometimes falls on receptive ears and sometimes it doesn't."

The male Cur smiled weakly. "And you had the proper equipment to show the Russians where and when they needed to fire the missiles?"

"Give me some credit, will you? I carry with me the same model Frumpian space-time directional simulator as you do and I also managed to get my hands on a slightly-used Klucktonian xaxomatic low-level energy reader, miniaturized, of course."

"But how did you know I was here? And why would you commit a deliberate act of disobedience by coming to Earth? Everyone (present planet excepted, of course) understands the consequences of willful disobedience."

She sighed deeply, and took a few moments to answer. "Well, you know, you're right. Maybe I should not have done this. Anyway, in answer to your first question, the Zurkidians told me what happened. One of their probes apparently spotted your shuttlecraft headed this way. I'm sorry, but I gave this thing a lot of thought. I concluded that I couldn't bear to be separated from you for eternity. And yes, I know that this body is now subject to physical death."

She paused. "What's going to happen to us? You know, ultimately. Is there salvation available to, excuse the expression, aliens?"

The male Cur, again appearing somewhat annoyed, quickly pulled his wife aside. He looked both directions to make sure they were out of hearing range. "Hold it," he whispered sternly. "You know as well as I do that there are certain things we can't discuss in front of the humans."

Then, turning back towards the crowd, "Look, if you folks don't mind, it's been a tough day, and my wife and I haven't seen each other for a long time. We'd like a little time alone."

Someone shouted, "I don't blame you Cur, from the neck down she's a real looker!"

The two Curians pretended not to hear, brushed aside a few last questions from reporters and ascended the rope ladder into the female Cur's space-craft.

As they climbed inside, she asked her husband, "What's this paper I found taped to the side of my ship?"

With a look of disgust, well known to the inhabitants of this world, he replied, "It's a ticket for illegal parking and noise pollution."

His wife appeared astonished. "I just risked my life saving the Earth from destruction, not to mention several people right here, and some minion of the law fined me for two questionable violations of local ordinances. What kind of place is this?"

The male Cur smiled broadly. "Relax, I have friends who will loan us the appropriate medium of exchange to pay for this."

In an instant, they disappeared into the sunset.

For the next several weeks, no one, not even Bill and Mildred Green, heard from the Curs. The two obviously had quite a bit of catching-up to do.

The comet however, which was now passing the Earth without incident, shone brightly in the night sky.

Epilogue

LIVING IN AMERICA

A YEAR HAD PASSED. Bill, Mildred, Rob, Sara, and the two Curs were gathered in the aliens' apartment to celebrate the anniversary of Mrs. Cur's landing and the redirection of the comet. The mood was festive as good friends reminisced about the events that brought them all together.

Following the female Cur's appearance, the two aliens discussed at great length how they might best spend the remainder of their now-finite natural lives. It was decided that, as long as they were now permanent inhabitants of this world, they might as well live among the humans.

Bill and Millie introduced them to a realtor, who rented them an apartment in northeast Philadelphia. Several of their human friends also donated cash to help the couple get started. The Curians, of course, insisted that they would pay this back.

Their new neighbors were initially not at all happy with this, and the realtor found himself the target of threats and vandalism for having moved aliens into the community. In the end however, most people concluded that the Curians were not so bad as long as they kept to themselves and could be tolerated provided that they did not bring any more Curians with them.

At his wife's prompting, the male Cur gave up being "The Mighty Cur" and gave his old uniform as a keepsake to Justin Black, a man who had twice saved his life. Black was appreciative, but confided to his family that he had no idea what he was going to do with it.

Cur instead started his own business transporting people between Philadelphia and New Jersey shore resorts. It was a struggle at first because, although these trips took less than a minute, many people were hesitant to ride in an alien spacecraft, and most senior citizens found it difficult to climb in and out of the top of the vessel.

Cur also discovered that, although his ship-board computers were more than sufficient for navigating the stars, they were utterly incapable of ensuring compliance with all of the federal, state, and local regulations that governed his business. He was thankful that he had not taken on any employees, for that would have required processing capabilities beyond anything known to exist in the galaxy.

The female Cur found herself in great demand, granting interviews and writing articles for several prominent magazines. Apparently a significant portion of the public wanted to know about alien women and what kind of men they preferred.

She rapidly fell out of favor with many women's groups however, because of her steadfast position regarding the sacredness of human life. She also found herself the center of much hostility and controversy, even in the churches, when she spoke about Curian family values. She soon learned not to make inflammatory statements such as, "Curian women respect their husbands."

Needless to say, the Curs found themselves subject to the normal strains of married life on Earth. Following a particularly heated discussion, the female Cur admitted that from the time she came to Earth she'd had an inexplicable urge to "straighten out" her husband, to force him to become something he's not.

In response, the male Cur confessed, "Don't feel bad Hon, I've got my own terrible urge—to sit around drinking intoxicating beverages and complaining to total strangers about how tough you are on me."

For the most part though, the Curs were growing stronger in gaining mastery over their strange new feelings and emotions. The only exception seemed to be on the golf course.

Meanwhile, Doctors Greed, Ego, and Pig were still influential and active within the world's various cultures, but there were also people courageous enough to fight the effects of their poison.

In any case, at the end of the evening, the three couples toasted their friendship, and Rob and Sara asked for their coats. Bill and Mildred remained behind for a few more minutes.

After his daughter and son-in-law had left, Bill turned to Cur (the male). "Do you remember the day you landed? During the ride back to my house, you told me that everyone in the universe knows about Earth and what they know is not good."

Cur laughed, "I'll never forget it."

Bill went on, "The human race owes you everything, but we've treated you pretty shabbily. What insufferable barbarians we must seem to you."

Cur shrugged. "What do you want me to say, Bill? I'm one myself now."

Bill smiled and got up, "Nothing you're not supposed to say, my friend."

As they walked towards the door, Bill turned and held up his hand. "Wait a minute, one more thing. I almost hate to bring this up because I know it's at the top of your forbidden list, but I'm going to come right out with it." The Curs said nothing, but seemed to expect what was coming next.

"You know Millie and I are Christians. Maybe we don't always live our faith the way we should, maybe we're not the best examples, but that's what we are, and…" His words trailed off as he watched the expressions on the faces of his extraterrestrial friends.

Cur (the female) took Bill's arm and pulled him closer. "You know, you Christians are too much. You drive me crazy!"

The male Cur tried to stop his wife, but she ignored him and went on.

"Let me tell you a little secret. You have no idea what you've got. You have the greatest message in the universe, and you act like it's something to be embarrassed about!"

The male Cur maneuvered himself between his wife and Bill, but she was not to be dissuaded. "Let me tell you something else I'll bet you didn't know. With all of the benefits enjoyed by all of the races we've mentioned during our times together, any member of any one of them would give anything in exchange for the privilege of being a Christian on Earth."

An awkward silence followed. Then Bill grunted a half-laugh. "You're kidding, right?"

He turned again towards the door, but the evening wasn't over quite yet.

Cur (the female) laughed softly. "Wait a minute. Look, I'm sorry, but I'm not exactly myself these days."

Bill and Millie thought it a little strange that her husband now had a huge grin on his face. They had seen him smile many times before, but never quite like this.

She took a deep breath. "Cur and I are about to become parents again."

To order additional copies of

THE CUR SONG

an alien's quest for meaning on the strangest planet in the universe

Bob Lockyer

send $10.99 plus $3.95 shipping and handling to

Books Etc.
PO Box 4888
Seattle, WA 98104

or have your credit card ready and call

(800) 917-BOOK